THE GYPSY & THE COUNT

1920

Aanya

The Bloodancer

DMITRI ENGELHARDT

RUSSIAN COUNT OF KALININGRAD

Lotte Engelhardt

Russian Countess

GYORGI

THE FIDDLER

Hanzi

The Trickster

JAINA

THE SEER

Tatyana Krupina

West Russian Peasant

Mila Nikolaevna

East Russian Peasant

ONAS

THE FIGHTER

CLAUDE ST. PIERRE

FRENCH CAPITAINE

RABBI ILYA USTIMOVICH

FENNIX THE STORYTELLER

Wilfred von Behrend

German Prinz

YOSKA

THE LIAR

"Everytime I Hear Thunder It Reminds Me Of You."

~ Dmitri

1

The revelation of Aanya's parentage still wasn't sitting well with her a week into the new year. She had come to terms with Jaina's lifelong lie and accepted the gypsy woman for what she had done. Aanya held nothing against the woman. There was a cloud of shame that followed her everywhere she went, which was mainly only her tent in camp these days. But Aanya had questions for her father. Wilfred couldn't have been as ignorant to her existence as he claimed to be. And she'd been there to see the shock on his face, but she wanted to exchange words with the man. For five years now he'd called Russia home, and she knew next to nothing about him except for the fact that he was crooked, corrupt, and crude. Jaina wasn't so inept as a human being to value such qualities in a man. There had to be something in him that she admired, that she cared for and curated within him. There had to be something redeemable. Even if he was a lifelong sinner, there was moments of sainthood. Aanya needed to cling onto those if she was to make peace with who she was, because the Wilfred that the public knew was an abhorrent figure, and his daughter wasn't much better.

Lotte was grappling with her own set of issues as the new year began. She too was content with the current state of affairs, but clueless as to how to go about fixing them. For starters, she was going insane inside Dmitri's apartment in the city. Even keeping separated on two different floors from her disgraced father wasn't enough to get by. He fell into drunken fits at least three times a week, which resulted in one broken window, three broken chairs, and a front door that hung awkwardly in its frame. The Red Army was as vigilant as ever in their posts outside the apartment. All doors and windows were accounted for at all times of the day and night. There was no room for error since their German origins made them a flight risk for the Bolsheviks. They were of low priority for formal imprisonment, and unfit for labor camps up in Siberia. There were rumors in the market that they might be traded back to Germany in exchange for some Russian prisoners of war which had been held captive for almost six years in some cases. But money issues always trumped rumors. The Bolsheviks needed resources to fund their civil war efforts. If the von Behrends could be ransomed, they might be worth keeping after all. Lotte was dark skinned and her reputation tainted as a future ex-Countess, but she was still young and useful. She could bare children for a general of the Red Army and turn her life around. Lotte wasn't fond of these options though, and contemplated suicide more in the past week than in her entire life.

With Dmitri's support Aanya was going to try and visit his apartment today to get some much-needed answers and closure. With a not so indulgent Mila being left behind in the forested camp, Claude volunteered his services as a public distraction. The new couple were teary eyed in their parting with Mila wishing Claude to exercise extreme caution while he was in the city today. The peace ambassador was overly confident in his horse-riding skills and ability to outsmart whatever government troops might be moving around Petrograd's icy streets this afternoon. Aanya and Dmitri were traveling on foot together, and left before Claude since he'd be faster. The friends met up just outside the far end of the Peter the Great Bridge, where Claude began to put on a wonderful, hair raising performance of showmanship. By shooting a pistol into the air and rearing his black horse up on its hind legs, he got the attention of all the Red Army soldiers guarding Dmitri's apartment. There was a defensive stance taken, and then a momentary pause to try and figure out what it was this black man was trying to do. If he was just causing a scene, the men shouldn't engage him, but if he posed a threat to the public, then they had a responsibility to protect the people. It was an indecisive back and forth for a few panicked seconds before the commanding officer of the day, a recently promoted young man, made the call to give chase to Claude. From her upstairs window Lotte could see Claude's show and was going to use that as her opportunity to escape the apartment with little else but the dress on her shoulders, but Wilfred was in the living room, draining the liquor cabinet.

"And just where do you think you're running off to, Lotte?"

"The men have been called out into the streets. This is my chance to be rid of you and this entire mess you've drug me into."

"There's no running from me."

"I have to try."

"I'll be sure to drag your body back into the apartment before it gets too desecrated."

"Desecrated?"

"Just what kindness are you expecting to be shown out there? There's not a soul in Petrograd who doesn't know who you are, *Countess*."

"The only thing I ever did wrong in life was listen to you. Once I'm on my own, and people see me for who I am…"

"They still won't like what they see. And if they have the unfortunate experience of having to listen to you talk, then you're in even more trouble."

"I can't live here with you anymore."

"You either live here with me, or you live nowhere."

"Is that a threat, father?"

"It is our reality. Yours and mine."

"I don't want this reality."

"Life doesn't care what you want."

"I want out though. I *will* get out, and I *will* be all the better for it. You can drink yourself to death here, but I will not watch your descent into chaos anymore. I want no part of you."

"I am half of you, whether you like it or not. I am all you know in this world. You will never survive away from me. I am your spine, your brain, and your confidence."

"I will find someone to help me."

"The only people known to care for the worthless in society are the worthless themselves. The gypsies. Will you go and beg your sister for help?"

"Aanya is not, and never will be my sister."

"You keep telling yourself that while you rot in the gutter."

"I am not as useless as you think I am."

"Go on then. Prove me wrong. Walk out that door. Because once you do, I will *never* welcome you back inside."

Lotte had hot tears burning in her eyes. She could not speak anymore because she was unable to choke back the pain of the truth in his words. He was drunk, yes, but he was being honest. Drunkards didn't possess the ability to lie. Wilfred had hit rock bottom weeks ago and therefore had no benefits to keeping cordial anymore. Grabbing a fistful of her last remaining fur coat, Lotte flung herself out the front door and made sure to slam it as hard as she could behind her. Now the paranoia of her new reality set in. Everyone was an enemy. The people on the street would scorn her. The police would arrest her. The soldiers, rape came to her mind and she wrapped her arms around herself for protection. There was no clear direction for her to walk in. No former friend's home was there for her peace of mind. She'd been disowned by all in high society, the few who remained and hadn't converted to the Bolshevik rhetoric. Her East Prussian home was not an option of comfort either. She had no money on her to even buy a train ticket had it been an option. She could see her jewelry that she wore. Her necklace would be worth something, and she traced her fingertips across the rounded jewels. This wasn't the life she ever thought she'd be living. To be utterly alone in this world. Alone in a crowd of people hurriedly rushing past her to work, market, or school. They had no time for her stalling at the intersections when they crossed the heavy thoroughfares. Around the block it still sounded like Claude was giving the soldiers hell, and it brought a slight grin to her face. She thanked him silently as a pair of copper hands landed on the back of her shoulders. She shrieked by accident as she jumped to see it was none other than her half-sister, Aanya. And with a protective arm around the gypsy's waist, Dmitri was standing there statuesque. There was a calmness about him Lotte had never seen before. The man looked comfortable. Like his place had always been beside Aanya. Lotte was slow in processing all of this. The gypsy recognized the Countess was having an episode of some sort, and tried to be patient, but still urged her to a nearby alley for some much-needed privacy. Laundry was hanging in a mass of lines here and to be concealed was quite easy. Among the lines of damp bedsheets Lotte was able to swallow her fears and recompose herself, a bit. Aanya went to let go of the younger woman but in an instant, and maybe unintentionally, Lotte's bloodshot eyes led her to grip onto Aanya's rotten green bracelet. Aanya yanked back instinctively to avoid another parting with it and Dmitri got in-between the two women before an altercation occurred. Lotte seemed surprised by her own behavior and then bowed her head.

"I'm so sorry, to the both of you. I didn't mean to grab you like that, Aanya. It's just been a difficult day for me."

"I was just playing it safe, Lotte. The last time you got a hold of me like that, I lost this bracelet."

"If I had known how important that was to you, to the both of you, I never would have taken it in the first place. It wasn't right."

"You're genuinely sorry, aren't you, Lotte?"

"Yes, Aanya. I am."

"You've been crying."

"I left my father this morning. *Our* father."

"Left him?"

"He's become a dangerous drunk lately, and I knew if I stayed in that apartment any longer, I'd…"

"You'd what?"

"I'd end up killing myself."

"While you are one of my least favorite people in the world, Lotte, I can't stand for you falling to such deep depths this quickly."

"It is my own hole that I've dug. And I will get myself back out of it."

"Don't blame yourself for what your father put you through."

"I was complicit for years. It's not like I haven't had a conscience this entire time. I know right from wrong. I know what liberties I've taken in life, and what I shouldn't have taken. I deserve my punishments, but I don't deserve torture. And that's what it has been like on house arrest."

"Where will you go, Lotte?"

"I don't know yet. This is all so new to me. I was hoping after walking around for a bit, something would just come to me."

"It's not safe for you to be walking the streets of Petrograd. The Reds are all over this city and the Whites are only getting closer. The Greens are in the forests. We're all surrounded. This escape you're looking for, it's not just going to come upon you, Lotte. You're going to have to hunt it down and fight for it. And I don't mean to add to your depressing state of affairs but I don't think you have it in you to make it through this."

"So new to the family yet I've already disappointed you. You're more of a von Behrend than I am."

"I will never be a von Behrend."

"You are who you are, Aanya. Your eyes give you away. What are you even doing here today? I saw your man on the horse run by earlier."

"I was hoping to speak to Wilfred."

"A fool's errand."

"I've done worse things before."

"I'd strongly advise you to abandon this task. The man is not very conversational these days."

"He might be for me."

"He'll just tear you to pieces."

"Then I'll tear into him too."

"This is not a battle worth fighting, Aanya. Please, don't go to the apartment."

"Is this what it looks like when you're trying to show concern for someone?"

"It is somewhat of a foreign concept for me. But I do pity your bloodline as much as my own. I do not wish for you to have any more hardships. I've caused enough grief for you over the years, let me at least try to redeem myself."

"One good deed does not undo a lifetime of bad."

"But it could be a step in the right direction."

"It could be. Or it could be nothing more than a slight misstep."

"I'm done misstepping."

"And all it took was a couple weeks of house arrest with old daddy dearest, huh? Dmitri, we should have tried this on your wife years ago."

"*Ex*-wife. Soon enough."

"When will the final papers be settled, Dmitri?"

"My lawyer said sometime this Spring, Lotte, at the latest. I'm waiting for a telegram any day now."

"And might I ask what will become of me when we are no longer entangled by law?"

"You will be as you were when I first brought you here. You'll be a German Prinzessin. You will be responsible for your own accounts, be they negative or positive. Once the Bolsheviks decide what to do about your father, and the house arrest is over, the apartment is as good as sold."

"It's like I never existed to you. You must feel so relieved to be free of me."

"I am relieved. But it does not make me happy to see you so dejected right now."

"It is only momentary I assure you."

"You don't have to pretend to be strong anymore. Everyone is only looking to you to see how far you fall before you accept your lot in life."

"I will never accept it. I will fight until the bitter end. I have to. I owe it to myself."

"Like Aanya, I don't mean to be condescending, but I don't think this is a fight you can win on your own. You're so ill equipped for this kind of life."

"I will adapt."

"How?"

"I don't know. When you brought me to Russia, I didn't know how I was going to survive, but I managed quite well for a few years."

"You were skating by on your father's influence, and riding on my coattails. You didn't gain anything on your own. You will not gain anything on your own in this new Soviet state either."

"Don't underestimate me, Dmitri."

"I'm not judging you, Lotte. I'm just trying to be honest with you, for your own good. I don't want to see this city eat you alive. And it will. It won't even take that long. You don't have to do this alone."

"Is this you offering to help me?"

"No. That's not my place. Aanya is in charge out in the forest. If she wants to help you, it's her hand you're going to have to take."

"I will not beg a gypsy to help me."

"You don't need to beg, Lotte. We gypsies help those in need. We're generous, but we're not doormats. We have respect for ourselves, and dignity. If you want help, all you need to do is ask. The time to swallow your pride is now, if that's the case."

"It's not the case."

"Then good luck navigating the wilds of Petrograd right now. It is not a place I would wish to traverse on my own."

"We are not the same, you and I."

"No. No, we're not. But we're not entirely that different either. You're a pretty young woman, Lotte, and you have a lot to offer the world still. Don't let them take everything that's good from you."

"You're foolish enough to think there's still something in me worth taking?"

"I do."

"Why do you think that?"

"I share half of my blood with you. I'm no part weakness. Family has to look out for one another, because at the end of the day, sometimes that's all you have left."

"If family has to look out for one another, then would you listen to me if I wanted to protect you?"

"I would consider your advice before acting."

"Then consider this, the both of you, get out of Russia while you still can. Petrograd isn't safe anymore."

"Offering me my own advice?"

"Dmitri will go wherever you do, Aanya. And while you and I may have no love loss for one another, I think we can both agree that Dmitri is a good man who deserves a good life."

"I will agree with you on that."

"Then get him out of here. Take him far, far away, and don't ever come back."

"Why do you say such things, Lotte?"

"I've listened in to one too many of my father's meeting with the Bolsheviks. The life they have planned for Russia, it's not one for the faint of heart. I may be ruined, and you may be nothing more than a gypsy, but Dmitri is an important man."

"I will keep him safe, Lotte. You have my word."

"Thank you, Aanya."

"You're welcome."

"Look at that! We *can* be civil towards one another. And to think, I've spent every day of the last five years hating you."

"Why was that, anyway?"

"You had what I always wanted. Dmitri."

2

For two long days Lotte had been trying to make a new life for herself in Petrograd. It was not going well. The first night she was able to sell her necklace to an old man for room and board. But on the second night when he came to her for a more intimate form of payment, she ran into the streets with her fur coat and settled for the shelter of an alley. After nearly freezing to death overnight, and starving, she worked a deal with the Red Army soldiers to let her back into the apartment. The deal entailed selling herself to the officer of the day. She had no intention of following through on her words though. She'd think of something before the shift change at noon in which her promise would be called upon. For now, all she could manage to do was cram stale bread into her face and drink half a pot of cold tea that Wilfred had forgotten about. He could be heard upstairs getting ready for the day. She wasn't ready to admit defeat to him, so she stole away in the downstairs library, and pretended not to exist.

In the gypsy camp on the outskirts of town, Lotte's demise was not coming as sweetly to Aanya's thoughts as she once would have liked. Dmitri appeared to be as calm as ever with the recent change of events. He'd settled into his new forest routine like it was second nature. In the afternoon he enjoyed going on walks with Ruslo to gather kindling for the fires at night. The little red fox hunted rabbits hibernating in their snow packed burrows for hours during the day. Simple things like this brought the former Count immense amounts of joy. Aanya couldn't help but feel like the man was ready to be a father. She swallowed hard at the thought of potentially disappointing him. She'd kept the truth of her pregnancy and subsequent miscarriage a secret from everyone in the world except Yoska. She couldn't break Dmitri like that. He wanted children with her, and she might not be able to give that to him. The thought of her turning out no better than Lotte was troubling. So, to rectify this karmic situation Aanya assumed that if Lotte's luck turned around, then maybe hers would turn around in the future as well. Where one shows kindness in the face of adversity, the same kindness will be shown unto them in a time of need. It is something Jaina once preached, when she used to be herself. Now she resigned to a life of reclusivity in her common-colored canvas tent. Never to be disturbed, never to contribute. Jaina was killing herself by being so withdrawn, but she was choosing this life. It had not been forced upon her. Taking advantage of Dmitri being busy, and Claude on patrol, Aanya slipped out to the Green Army camp for Yoska's help.

"Not that I'm not excited to see you, Aanya, but your face has me worried."

"You know sometimes I wish you weren't such a good reader of people, Yoska."

"I'm not a good reader of people. I'm just a good reader of you. Now slow down and stop fidgeting. You're safe in the Green camp."

"I'm safe nowhere, but I appreciate your coddling. I need you to help me with something."

"Something bad or else you'd have your men in camp help you. I don't see Dmitri and Claude anywhere behind you. You came here alone?"

"I won't be leaving alone. You'll help me, won't you?"

"I hate that you know I can't turn you down. One thing before you get into the details, is this going to be dangerous?"

"Potentially."

"Alright, let me try wording that a little bit differently. Aanya, will I need to be bringing a gun with us today?"

"Yes."

"So, it is dangerous."

"Danger is a matter of perspective."

"No, not really."

"I need you to help me get Lotte out of Petrograd."

"Why on earth would I want to help you do that?"

"She's my half-sister."

"That's new. But if her mother was an African, and you're a gypsy, that means your father…"

"Yes. Yes, it's true. We don't need to keep saying that unfortunate little tidbit out loud for more ears to hear."

"My condolences."

"Thanks."

"That explains some things though."

"What things?"

"Why you're so hard headed."

"My apologies."

"No need. I always liked the fact that you were a strong-willed woman. You know what you want and you go after it. I'm excited by the fact you even came out to me today, that you still want me in your life."

"I'll always want you in my life. But right now, I'm more interested in using your skillset."

"What skills might you be referring to?"

"Breaking and entering?"

"And kidnapping?"

"It's for her own good. I have the worst feeling that something bad is going to happen to her. I've had it for two days now and it's only getting worse. She said she left her father, but I know she's gone back. She had no other choice."

"Blood or not, I just can't help but feel you're going to regret this."

"Why?"

"She'd never go so far to save you."

"I'm alright with that. She'll come to terms with our shared parentage in her own time. But until that day comes, I need to show her what a good older sister is capable of. She's the only sibling I have."

"Aanya?"

"What?"

"Are you trying to save Lotte today because you weren't there when Gyorgi was killed?"

"What's wrong with wanting to help those in need?"

"Nothing."

"So, are you going to grab your guns or what?"

"I'm sorry. *Guns*? As in plural?"

"One for you, one for me."

"What's your experience with a gun?"

"If I need to kill a man today, I want protection."

"You're being reckless. And while that's something I usually find extremely attractive about you; I will not be risking your neck for the likes of Lotte. I'll bring two guns, but I'm keeping them both on me. I'm all the protection you'll be needing today."

"But what happens if we get separated?"

"We *won't* be getting separated."

"Things go wrong all the time, Yoska. We very well may be separated."

"No. I won't let that happen. You're sticking by my side and that's all there is to it."

"And you call *me* hard headed."

"Hey, I learned it from you."

"Are you insinuating that I'm a bad influence?"

"The worst. It's a good thing you're pretty though."

"Has my appearance blinded your better judgement all these years?"

"I didn't have any better judgment to start out with. I just wanted an excuse to tell you that you're pretty."

"Always the charmer."

"What can I say? You bring out the best in me."

"Before we go, is there some commanding officer in the Green Army that you need to report to? I don't want to be the reason you get in trouble."

"I don't report to anybody in life. And if I did, it'd be you, Aanya."

"Then let's get out of here. The sooner we can get Lotte back to camp, the better."

"What's the rush?"

"I didn't tell anyone what I was doing today."

"Of course not. Are Claude and Dmitri going to attack me for being your accomplice later?"

"Don't worry. I won't let them hurt you."

Aanya took hold of Yoska's brown vest and tugged him behind her in a half run towards Petrograd. Yoska had never so willingly followed anyone into harm's way before, but for Aanya he'd run into a firing squad. She had been justified to come to him in her time of need. Not only was he unable to turn her down, but he was the perfect man for the job. He was also always up for a challenge, and going up against a team of Red Army soldiers was right up his alley. He got a thrill about what could be awaiting him when he crossed the bridge. Aanya's feet never slowed and never faltered. She was going to get Lotte out of that apartment, and she was going to do right by a woman who had done nothing but wrong to her. Blood or not, Yoska couldn't understand the sudden tinge of sentimentality here, but as far as trying to make amends for Gyorgi's death, he'd say no more. Her eyes glistened with tears the entire morning. Her emotions were running almost dangerously high. It could either help her or hurt her, and if the latter came true, Yoska had come to terms with the fact that this might be his last adventure with Aanya the Bloodancer. Just before they crossed the bridge, he stopped cold in his run and tugged Aanya backwards into his chest. He wrapped his arms around her back and she didn't pull away when he slammed his lips down into hers. That was a good sign. And they lingered in hold for longer than a mere fraction of a second before Yoska finally got a hold of himself and released her.

"I just needed to feel that high one more time."

Aanya nodded then sprinted off again with her gypsy in tow. If she had words in her head right now, she didn't say them. Yoska took the lead now midway across the bridge. The rescue mission had begun. The Red Army officer blew a whistle to alert his fellow wool coats to the threat of an attack. They converged on the front door of the apartment, and for the first time in hours Lotte came out of her hiding place in the downstairs library. She met her father at the front window who was too much in a drunken stupor to fully gather everything that was happening. He vaguely gestured something beside her on the velveted sofa, but she paid him no mind. Her eyes were focused on Aanya and Yoska in the street. It had come to an almost immediate standoff. Nine to two. The tenth man was walking back to the front door right now. After the third bang Wilfred became so annoyed by the sound, he got up to answer it. The young man in uniform had come for orders, and was asking for permission to shoot. Wilfred not only gave permission, but also insisted on following the gypsy couple all the way back to their camp, and killing the lot of them. Only Jaina was to be spared, and brought back here by any means necessary. Lotte angrily mustered what little strength she had left in her and tried to intervene but the tenth man had promptly left the door by the time she arrived. Then Wilfred proceeded to add insult to injury by shoving past his daughter so hard they both tumbled to the ground.

"I thought I said that you weren't welcome back?!"

"Don't worry, father. I was just leaving."

Wilfred again vaguely gestured towards his daughter and then began the struggle to upright himself with the aid of a broken chair he'd mangled the night before in a drunken rage. Lotte was frantically clawing at the wooden floors for her own support as she got back up on her feet and scrambled outside. Yoska had Aanya behind him for protection, a gun in each hand. It was surely going to be the death of them both in a matter of seconds. Their eyes were cold to the truth. Not warm fog of air escaped their closed mouths or noses. Lotte heard the Red Army officer give the order to shoot to wound, so that they may be able to follow the injured back to the forest and kill the rest of them. Aanya sneered in defiance. It might be her last move in this world. She would be killed for sure. They didn't need both gypsies alive, and her clawed hand on Yoska's shoulder was white knuckled now. Lotte saw everything as it happened, only slower. She wasn't even intentionally acting on her own accord anymore as she pushed through the group of soldiers. She was nearly incapacitated by the jolt of action to her weak system, but her body was pure adrenaline at this point. A firefight had started. Aanya had surged forwards to protect Yoska while he shot himself out of bullets in a hurry. Aanya danced through gunfire like she was magic. Lotte got up to her feet and was instantly caught in the crosshairs as she reached out for her sister. Lotte was shot in the back, and bleeding profusely as the bullet seemed to tear straight through her organs and lodge itself in her gut. As she collapsed on her face Aanya was there to pull her up into her lap. Yoska was fighting with his fists now, but neighbors who'd secretly been watching the whole thing go down now came out in support of the gypsies and against the Red Army men who'd been terrorizing them for months. A man from across the street was even kind enough to help carry a dying Lotte up into the back of one of his fruit carts so they could ride out towards the safety of the forest. Ten dead Red Army soldiers had fallen in the street, and nobody needed to be around when the police showed up. Yoska drove the cart out across the Peter the Great Bridge while Aanya sat on the floor of the carriage with the extra fabric of her skirts balled up to soak up the blood leaking out Lotte's back. The dark-skinned beauty would never make it to camp, but what was more important was that she didn't die near her father. Aanya kept squeezing the young woman's hand but Lotte couldn't squeeze back.

"It's going to be alright, Lotte. We're going to get you sewn back up and we're going to fix all of this alright? You're going to be just fine."

"Don't lie to me, Aanya."

"I'm not lying."

"I'm so cold."

"Don't worry. I'll get you out by the fire when we get to camp. That will warm you right up. Just a little bit longer now. I need you to hang onto me, alright? Just hang on, Lotte. Yoska's going as fast as he can."

"How do you do it?"

"How do I do what?"

"Yoska would do anything for you."

"No, he wouldn't."

"He almost died for you. I saw the way, the way he jumped up and held you back. He'd die for you. No one's ever loved me like that. No one will *ever* love me like that now."

"No, Lotte. No! Stay with me! Come on!"

"I don't want to fight this."

"I'll fight for you. What are sisters for, huh?"

"Don't be nice to me just because I'm dying. I don't deserve it."

"You don't know what you deserve or not. Just wait. There's a whole life you've got ahead of you."

"I can't feel my legs, Aanya!"

"Yoska, drive faster!"

"I'm trying! Is anybody behind us?"

"I don't know!"

"Aanya?"

"Yes, Lotte?! I'm right here. What do you need? What do you want? What can I do for you?"

"I'm so scared!"

"It's going to be alright. It's going to be alright. I'm right here."

"Don't leave me."

"I'm not going anywhere. I'm right here."

"The sun's in my eyes. It hurts."

"The sun? There's no sun out today. It's cloudy."

Aanya looked up in confusion, but in her arms, she could feel Lotte's body fall limp. The young woman was still staring up aimlessly into the sky when Aanya dropped her gaze back down. Aanya tried shaking her a couple of times to prolong the inevitable, but it was done. Lotte had lost too much blood to survive. Yoska was still barreling out to the forest like a madman when Aanya yelled for him to stop. There was a brief pause before the fruit cart slowed to the side of the dirt path. Yoska was quick to get back to the women, and try and figure out what needed to be done next. It was quickly decided that Lotte would be buried in the already hallowed ground of the old gypsy camp, where Gyorgi had been buried as well. Aanya and Yoska dug the grave with their hands since the earth was soft enough with all the wet weather. It was dirty work, but it was worth the effort. Lotte had jumped in front of them to take a bullet that would have resulted in severe tragedy. Had Aanya been killed, the rippling effects would have been catastrophic. Had Yoska been killed, Aanya would have been numb for an eternity. This way, the gypsies had been spared. They'd been spared by a woman that up until just a few days ago despised their entire people to her core. The commotion at the road caught Claude's eye first, who then alerted Mila, who got a hole of Dmitri still out in his firewood walk. The rest of camp was left to their own devices for privacy. Claude reached the grave first and help conceal Lotte before Mila and Dmitri ran up out of breath. It was an unspoken knowledge that the former Count did not need to see the face of his dead wife. The mound of dirt was completed and patted down by the time Dmitri came to the edge of the road. He angrily eyed Yoska at first like he was going to start raging, and Yoska quietly dropped his head to take the lashing, but Aanya stepped in-between them, with her back against Yoska's chest, and let her hand slip down to wind her fingers around the gypsy man's. Dmitri cooled, and she rose her free hand to his chest. After shaking her head no, Dmitri began to break down. He dropped to his knees and Mila began to whimper in Claude's arms out of sympathy for her former employer turned friend. Aanya tried soothing him as best she could.

"She died saving us, Dmitri. Please don't be angry with her. She's finally escaped her troubles."

3

Saturday, 10th January

It was early in the morning when the sounds of horse's hooves thundered off in the distance of the forest. The men on patrol were quick to take a defensive approach and stand guard, but when it became clear that they were outnumbered and outgunned they closed back in on the safety of the safety of the camp. The tents on the outskirts scattered inwards first, slowly but surely waking up everyone in the process. Within three minutes everyone was awake and startled. Dmitri had a terrible headache from crying over Lotte's death which had only happened hours earlier. Aanya insisted he stay behind in the tent while she came out to assess the situation but he would not be held back or away from her. Claude was discussing the specifics with the men who'd been out on patrol while Yoska ran in from the Green Army camp who were already alerted to the fact that the Reds were moving in thick and fast. It was a different band of

Red Army soldiers though than the ones Aanya had befriended in the forest. They were still sound asleep and silent as the grave. That didn't make any sense why one band of Reds wouldn't have alerted the other to their activities unless this was something urgent or covert. Aanya had a sinking feeling in her stomach that Yoska's wide eyes only intensified. Wilfred's threat to have the entire gypsy camp killed was about to be fulfilled. Aanya looked around at three hundred pairs of eyes all staring at her. She swallowed hard and realized only one person's eyes were quiet in all of this, her mother's. Jaina was oddly calm in all of this chaos. She was sitting just outside her tent, open eyed and meditating with crossed legs. She knew something. She'd seen this and chosen not to say anything. By morning things would be very different. Aanya took action while she had the chance and began barking orders in a stern and steady voice. Claude and Mila were going on horseback to lead the gypsies to the Moscow band's abandoned campgrounds. This was only temporary. Claude would take the long way around. The peace ambassador grabbed Mila and a bag from their tent before falling in line down the dirt road. The carts and wagons were being loaded, horses harnessed and sacks packed. It was automatic and it was lightning fast. In five minutes, everyone was moving away to safety. Aanya was not leaving. Instead, she was going to meet the Red Army force face to face on the road. Yoska pressed a long rifle into her hands as she passed him. This time he'd brought two guns, and gave her the better one. She kissed his cheek as the two parted and Dmitri walked over to his rival.

"That's *my* girl, Yoska."

"No, that's *our* woman, Dmitri."

"I know she's keeping something from me right now. Do you know what it is?"

"She'll tell you everything you need to know when you need to know it."

"What happened in the city today?"

"Nothing good."

"Why is the Red Army coming out here?"

"You can thank your father-in-law for that."

"Why was he provoked?"

"Since when did that man need to be provoked to be a jerk?"

"You make a good point."

"There was a shootout at your apartment. Between your neighbors and I, we killed the ten Red Army guards that had been on duty there."

"So, we're at war with the Reds then?"

"I guess you could say that."

"Well thank you for running out here to tell us. But I'm sure the Greens will be wanting you back."

"No. My place is here with Aanya. Until I know she's safe, I'm not going anywhere. She already sent Claude and Mila away. The people will be safe following them, but this is her home. She's going to need my help defending it."

"It's not like she was going to be here alone. I'm staying here with her too."

"Good. Then she'll have twice the protection."

"Is this the way it's going to be now?"

"What do you mean?"

"I don't want to share her with you."

"Likewise. But what man she chooses is her decision and her decision alone."

"I'm here now."

"For good?"

"Yes!"

"We'll see how long that lasts."

"I love Aanya, Yoska."

"I love her too, Dmitri. And don't you dare think that you love her more."

"You'd die for her?"

"I almost did this afternoon! But Lotte had a stroke of compassion spring up in her at the worst possible time. I did everything I could, Dmitri. Honest. Aanya and I didn't want your wife to die the way she did."

"Please stop calling her my wife, Yoska."

"But she was."

"We were as good as divorced as of the first of next month. She had to have known. I sent a telegram to the apartment. There was no sudden rush of compassion in her. She'd been looking for a way out for weeks."

"You think she let herself get shot?"

"You didn't know Lotte the way I did."

"And you weren't with her when she died. *I* was. And I know that woman wasn't ready to go out like that. Her and Aanya were going to work through things and try to be some kind of family."

"Those women would have killed each other before they ever reached a compromise."

"Give them more credit than that."

"I was. There was too much of their father in them. They couldn't help it."

"But Aanya had a good upbringing."

"You mean Jaina over there?"

"The woman isn't all bad."

"You look at her smiling face over there and tell me that's a good woman. She saw this coming, Yoska. She saw all of this and chose not to tell us. We could have been safe in Moscow by now had she gave us the proper warning."

"Like Moscow is safe."

"It's safer than Petrograd right now."

"And by morning that could all change. Russia is not safe. You can keep running from one fire to another, but you're still burning all the same."

"What's your brilliant solution then? What should we have done?"

"There is no brilliant solution to this war. And I'm not the idea man. I'm muscle. I'm brawn. Aanya's the brain here. Ask her. She's the only one with enough wherewithal to take action when the rest of us were all standing around scatterbrained."

"She's odd like that, isn't she?"

"She's amazing is what she is. I wish I had half the courage that woman did."

"She'd laugh at you if she heard you say that."

"Which is why I'm standing here talking to you."

"Why are you talking to me at all?"

"I'm trying to get a read on why Jaina's sitting there all calm like. Smiling like a damned fool."

"I know the woman. I already told you. She's seen this. She knows what's going to happen when the Reds storm this empty camp."

"And how do you know this?"

"She was like a mother to me. A child can read their mother."

"You're neither a child, nor is she your mother."

"Close enough."

"In what regard?!"

"I'm not going to argue with you, Yoska. Not tonight. It wouldn't do any good."

"Then you get Jaina to spill her guts so I can go out there and stand with Aanya, or I'm going to start at that woman with violent interrogations."

"Touch me and it'll be the last thing you ever do, Yoska!"

"So, you have been listening to us, Jaina?"

"Who else was I supposed to listen to? You two squawking back and forth like a couple of hens in the morning. Both of you should be ashamed of yourself! Leaving Aanya out by the road all by herself."

"You'd know all about being ashamed, wouldn't you, Jaina?"

"Yoska, I'm really not in the mood for your mouth right now."

"Well, are you in the mood for a confession or two? Because I'd like to know why you kept all of this to yourself."

"I didn't see any of this happening until a couple of hours ago. You know I can't see anything Aanya does when she's with you."

"Because when she's with me I'm all she can think about?"

"This is no time to build yourself up, Yoska."

"A man has to have fun sometime."

"Now is not the time. Just go and stand with Aanya and leave me with Dmitri."

"Wait, why do *I* have to stay behind, Jaina?"

"Because I need to speak to you, Dmitri. Go, Yoska!"

"Alright, alright! I'm going. I'm gone. I'd rather be holding onto Aanya anyways. You smell, Dmitri."

"I do not smell, Yoska!"

"No, Dmitri. He's right. You do smell."

"Like what, Jaina?"

"Anxiety…and salt. You've been crying. And you haven't slept at all tonight, have you?"

"I couldn't."

"Because of Lotte?"

"I didn't think divorcing her was going to kill her."

"You couldn't have saved that woman."

"It still shouldn't have ended like this."

"Everything happens the way it's supposed to happen, when it's supposed to happen. You understand me?"

"Why does it feel like you're saying goodbye to me, Jaina?"

"Because I won't be coming back out to the forest, Dmitri. And I want to make sure when I leave, that everything is going to be taken care of. I need to know Aanya's going to be taken care of."

"I won't let anything happen to her. I promise."

"She's all I have, Dmitri. My only child. My baby girl. I…I…"

"You don't owe me any sort of explanation. She'll be taken care of. But what's going to happen to you?"

"What needs to happen."

"You're not going to tell me anything more specific than that?"

"Details won't make it any easier for you to understand, Dmitri. I just wanted to thank you."

"Thank me for what?"

"Being there for my girl."

"Then I should apologize to you for all the years I wasn't here for her."

"You were here, even if not physically. She's never let go of you. Not even when I pushed her. She's always had a mind of her own, and I've loved her for that. I just don't need that to become her undoing."

"Aanya will be looked after. You have my word, Jaina. She will know how much you loved her. I'll remind her anytime she might doubt it."

"Will you help me one last time before the Reds arrive?"

"Yes. What do you need me to do?"

"I will be allowed one bag of my belongings, but I won't be needing much. Just a few things. A handful really. In Aanya's tent there is a red satchel full of herbs. Can you get that for me?"

"The whole thing?"

"Yes. All of it."

"But why do you need that if it's Aanya's?"

"It was mine before I left. It is the leader's responsibility to keep hold of it."

"They're poisonous, aren't they?"

"In case of an emergency they provide someone who is dying with instant comfort. Now please, Dmitri! Can you go and grab that satchel for me?!"

"You're planning on killing yourself, aren't you?"

"Grab the satchel!"

"I won't help you kill yourself!"

"I'm dying with or without your help!"

"I can't do this."

"Would you sleep better at night knowing I died in pain then? Severe, excruciating pain?"

"It doesn't have to be like this, Jaina."

"What do you know of what will come to be?! You can't see! You have not seen what I have seen!"

"There must be another way."

"There isn't. This must happen this way."

"Or what?"

"Would you sacrifice Aanya to save me?"

"That's my only alternative?"

"Let me die so that my daughter may live."

"The red satchel, you said?"

"Yes."

"She's going to notice it's missing."

"I will be dead before that happens."

While Dmitri grabbed the red satchel, he intentionally spilled half of the contents out onto the ground for good measure. Jaina was so frantic that she didn't seem to notice when she snatched it out of Dmitri's clammy hands. She then instantly apologized for her snappy behavior and pulled the former Count in for a hug. It was awkward and uncomfortable for both parties, but a necessary formality to get out of the way. Dmitri escorted Jaina by her arm out to the roadside where the first of the Red Army men were just now arriving in a billowing cloud of dust. Aanya stood strong and resolute with Yoska on the right of her and Dmitri on the left. Negotiations for sparing the camp quickly followed, much to Aanya's discontent. But to remain a firm leader she could not show duress or discomfort. With glistening eyes, she watched her mother offer herself up as a sacrifice to the Red Army. She was manhandled up onto the back of a horse, handcuffed ruthlessly, and gagged with one of her own blue scarves. Her golden piercings that looped from her nose to her ears were violently yanked out of place until she screamed bloody murder from the pain. Aanya had to be physically restrained at this point by both Dmitri and Yoska. Dmitri turned his back though. Hearing the harassment was bad enough, he didn't need to watch it too. Instead, he watched Yoska's facial expressions. The gypsy man was some kind of masochist. Stone faced while Jaina sat there being tortured. The herbs she swallowed hadn't yet taken effect but they would soon. The pulsating adrenaline in her body was speeding up the saturation in her blood. The Red Army men who had come out tonight were high leaders in the Bolshevik party. They could be discerned by their rotten green woolen jackets. Aanya spit on them as they rode away in another cloud of smoke. The whole encounter took less than ten minutes. Dmitri let Aanya go the second she tugged against his hold, but Yoska knew better than to give in so quickly. With only one arm restrained though she was a wild cannon, and was able to hold the long rifle up to her side and crank one shot out at the Red Army men running away. She didn't hit anyone, but it felt good for her to even try. Yoska only let her go now to wrench the gun out of her hands and empty the remaining bullets. As they jingled to the ground, he turned back to cast a scowl at Dmitri for letting go of her too soon.

"She could have hurt herself, Dmitri!"

"I trusted her! She knew what she was doing!"

"If she fucking shot one of them, they would have all ridden back and killed us where we stood!"

"Both of you be quiet! My mother needs my help! How are we going to get her back?"

"She's not coming back, Aanya."

"What are you talking about, Dmitri?"

"She said it was you or her. She's seen it."

"I'm *not* losing my mom and sister on the same day."

4

The corner apartment in Petrograd which Dmitri had rebuilt in his name was the current prison for disgraced German Prinz Wilfred von Behrend and his lover slash prisoner Jaina the Seer. The gypsy woman had not succumbed to fatal beatings, starvation, or various verbal harassment barrages. Wilfred was as guilty as the Red Army soldiers that guarded the residence. Jaina was berated on a nearly constant basis, but had taken up an effective coping mechanism to disassociate herself from this physical world. She had refrained from speakin, crying, or showing much in the way of emotion. She had become an object in the household, and little more. Wilfred drank with her, for her, and around her while the Red Army soldiers, which now made regular visits inside the apartment, took what they pleased, said what they pleased, and pleasured themselves as they pleased. It'd been the better part of six weeks in this new life for Jaina, and her body was beginning to fail her. The path to death was a long one.

Dmitri had received a telegram from Moscow yesterday that in order for his sale to go through on his apartment that the house arrest order against Wilfred was going to have to be settled within the week. The former Count had little negotiating power left to his name, and speaking to the Bolsheviks outright on their home turf was almost asking for suicide. Not to mention that fact that he refused to leave Aanya's side anymore. Anywhere they traveled, it had to be safe enough for both of them, or they didn't go. That also meant the arrangement Aanya had made with the Red Army camp in the forest had also been cancelled. She no longer danced for them in exchange for a handsome supply of cash and peace of mind. Claude had amped up patrols to combat that change. More men, bigger men, and guns on full display around the clock. It was like living in a military state, which really wasn't anyway to live at all. Camp was safe enough though, for now. The gypsies had returned from their rush out to Moscow. No loss of life had been reported because Aanya had taken action fast enough. She received much praise and respect for that. No one aside from Aanya herself seemed to have trouble with Jaina's sacrifice. She'd become so strange in the camp that her absence was actually preferred. But Aanya kept the woman's tent up regardless of the possibility of her ever returning. She knew Dmitri completely doubted the gypsy woman was even alive anymore, but Aanya would not give up so easily. That's why when he decided to make a visit to his apartment to try and work a deal with Wilfred about moving somewhere else for his house arrest, the entire group traveled with him. Claude for extra manpower, Mila because the couple was glued at the hip, and Yoska because he didn't trust Dmitri.

The negotiation in Dmitri's apartment turned into the strangest of dinner parties. It was early in the evening, but Wilfred had the dining room set up like a grand feast and ball was to be held that night. There were plates and crockery, utensils and empty glasses all strewn about. Jaina sat at one end of the table, like a ghost in human form. Her face was sucked in, her copper skin dull, and eyes blackened from beatings. Her face still bore the scars of her piercings having been ripped out upon capture almost two months ago. Her blue capes, skirts, and scarves hadn't been washed since her stay here. Her black hair had been cut, cropped short like a man's, and she couldn't have cared less. Aanya tried sharing brief moment with her mother under her breath but Aanya was only met with silence every time. The only way to get through these negotiations now was to play along with whatever game it was that Wilfred had convinced himself that he was living. He sat down at the head of the table, opposite Jaina, and the younger guests were to fill themselves in accordingly. There was no food being prepared or had. The only drink was in Wilfred's hand, but he slammed his fist down on the table everyone scrambled for a seat. Dmitri took Wilfred's left hand side, with Aanya sitting between himself and her mother. Opposite Dmitri, Claude sat down to Wilfred's right, then promptly placed a locked and loaded pistol on the table, pointed at the eccentric old man, with his finger on the trigger. Mila sat between Claude and Jaina, opposite Aanya. All Mila could do was sniffle and whimper at the extreme tension that hung in the air. Yoska was neither invited to the table, nor was he willing to squeeze in anywhere. Instead, he fashioned himself a standing defensive position behind Wilfred, and in front of the back door where four Red Army soldiers frequently eyed the copper skinned assassinator of their fellow soldiers six weeks ago. Wilfred held his shaking hand up to give a toast. He angrily cleared his throat until the rest of the patrons held up their empty, mismatched glassware accordingly, and stared at the old man. Jaina remained still, on the darker, unlit portion of the dining table. Apparently, that was alright as the Prinz gave a rambling and largely unintelligible speech about a prosperous new year. After clanking glasses and resuming a few seconds of awkward silence, Aanya reached down and grabbed Dmitri's hand beside her, and insisted the negotiations begin.

"Aanya, if you have something to say to me, speak up. I'm your father now after all. I'm sure there's much you'd like to discuss tonight."

"I actually don't have anything to say to you. But Dmitri does, don't you?"

"Yes, I do. Wilfred, it's come to my attention that your stay here is limited."

"And who told you that? Lenin? Trotsky maybe?"

"You know I sold this apartment last year, yes?"

"The Bolsheviks don't care what men like you or I do. They follow their own set of rules."

"Regardless, the apartment has been sold, and my buyer is under the full intention of moving in here on the first of the month."

"What day is it today?"

"The 24th."

"That gives me a week then."

"No. Wilfred that gives you the next four days to pack whatever belongings you may have managed to keep to your name, and be housed elsewhere."

"Where am I supposed to go?"

"That's your problem. Not mine."

"You only came to visit me to give me bad news?"

"I came as a courtesy to your past patronage to me in my youth. I owe you nothing. I could have just let the telegram I received pass me by and let this all come as a shock to you in four days. But in your age and declining health…"

"My *age* and *declining health*?!"

"You are not well, Wilfred."

"Can you even believe the way this boy is speaking to me, Jaina?! It is brash, is it not?"

"My mother's not going to answer you, Wilfred."

"Father! You call me father now, do you understand, Aanya?"

"I will *never* call you father. You're an abusive drunk and I'd like nothing more than to leave here as soon as possible and never have to look at you again."

"You're going to break your mother's heart saying things like that."

"I can't break what you've already broken."

"You don't know your mother as well as you think you do, Aanya."

"I know her better than you, Wilfred."

"You'd like to think so. But she's kept more secrets from you than she has from me."

"I don't know about that. She may have lied to me about being my mother, but she still raised me, and loved me, and guided me. She never abandoned me. She had two children with you and never even told you. I'd say her love for me is greater than whatever hold you have over her."

"If you're under the impression I'm holding her against her will then you're entirely mistaken. She is more than free to come and go as she pleases. Aren't you, Jaina? See? See how she sits there. She can't stand the thought of leaving me. She simply loves me too much."

"Nobody loves you too much. Nobody even loves you at all. The only person who might have ever loved you was Lotte. But she's dead."

"Lotte?"

"Yes, Wilfred. My sister is dead."

"That can't be."

"The soldiers shot her just outside the front door."

"You're lying! Lotte's been in Moscow for weeks."

"What are you talking about?! She was shot! I saw it happen. She took a bullet for me, to protect me."

"She hated you!"

"She died for me!"

"She did not!"

"Her blood stained my hands for weeks! Don't tell me it didn't happen!"

"Aanya, stop."

"No, Dmitri! I will not stop! He deserves to hear what I have to say."

"You're only making things worse."

"Like *you* were handling things any better."

"I was trying to keep everyone calm."

"Then you should have never brought me."

"I wasn't going to come without you."

"Then let me speak to my father the way he needs to be spoken to. This is a family affair anyway, and you're not family, Dmitri. Not according to law."

"Don't take your anger out on me, Aanya. I don't deserve it."

"You don't deserve to be sheltered from it either!"

"Dmitri, Aanya…"

"WHAT CLAUDE?!"

"Don't yell at him!"

"Mila you stay out of this!"

Chaos had consumed the dining room as Dmitri, Claude, Aanya, and Mila all consumed each other in a back-and-forth argument that included at least three of the four parties at any given time. There was no following one string of insults because too many were flying around at once. Through all of this yelling, shouting, screaming, and crying, Yoska stood impatiently at the back door in a stare down with one of the soldiers outside getting a little too cheeky with the trigger of his gun. Wilfred was laughing and quite pleased with himself at the head of the table, clapping and pointing in approval at various points being made in the onslaught of releasing the pressure which had been building for months, and in some attacks, years. He was particularly happy with some points Aanya made about loyalty, and that Claude made about respect. Mila was so upset most of her comments were overshadowed by the fact she was crying uncontrollably. Dmitri kept slamming his hands down on the table, trying to talk over everyone in a fatherly tone. When he hit the table though, it kept shuddering all the empty glassware, and in one case sent Jaina's glass smashing into the ground. Aanya bent down mid rage to pick up the pieces, then cut herself on a shard. Claude chastised her for not being more careful. Dmitri attempted to tend to her wound but she shoved him off, staining his shirt. This upset Mila who was still quite defensive of her former employer. This upset Claude because he was still feeling an inferiority complex over Mila's attachment to the former Count. Wilfred got up to refill his glass with more vodka and set the record player up again. In the background of this dinner party gone awry was the classical stylings of Modest Mussorgsky's 1867 masterpiece, Night on Bald Mountain. The orchestra providing the ambient music to this mental collapse seemed oddly appropriate. And deeper into the background, while everyone was consumed with another's inadequacies and intricacies, Jaina had unveiled the little red satchel she'd been hiding on her person for weeks. After inspecting the herbs slowly, and carefully, she wadded up a sprig of something and took care to chew it and swallow it was grace and poise. The sound of her incapacitated body slumping off of her chair and onto the hardwood floors was silence inducing. Jaina had committed suicide right there at the dinner table with all the audience in the world, and no one had even noticed until it was too late. Aanya dropped to the floor next, scraping her hands and knees up against the still broken glass. She didn't care now as Dmitri and Claude attempted to resuscitate the older gypsy woman to no avail. Mila propped the woman's head up in her lap. Yoska looked at the group, converging in spite of their former hatred, and then looked up at Wilfred, still standing by the record player, drinking his vodka with vile disinterest. This bottle had been watered down. Yoska picked up his gun and took aim at Wilfred only for the older man to laugh in response as the violins played on.

"I wouldn't do that if I were you, young man."

"And why wouldn't you?"

"You'll have the Reds rushing in here so fast you won't even have a chance to blink your eyes."

"I'll take my chances, Wilfred."

"You're funeral."

"You think after everything I've been through in the past five years that something like death can still scare me?"

"You'd never see my daughter again."

"Yoska?! Yoska put the gun down!"

"No, Aanya."

"Yoska, please!"

"This man doesn't deserve to breathe! Look at everything he's caused just today alone. Let me kill him. Let me end this for you."

"While I agree my father is a piece of human waste, he does not deserve the dignity of dying by your hand."

"You take mercy on him?"

"I do not. But this is what he wants. Don't give into his games. You are better than he is."

"You're almost as good at lying to men as your mother was, Aanya."

"You don't speak about my mother! You don't so much as utter her name anymore, you hear me, Wilfred?!"

"Or what, Aanya? *Or what*?!"

"I can get the men out in the street to kill you. They'd do just about anything for me."

"Do it then."

"Not today. You don't deserve a quick death. You deserve to sit with your thoughts, and realize what you've done. You need to take responsibility. Lotte is dead. Jaina is dead. Your son is dead. I'm all you have left in the world, and you don't even have me."

"I don't want you."

"Then what was this stupid dinner party for then? What were you trying to accomplish with all of this?"

"Who said I was trying to accomplish anything?"

"You're always trying to work some kind of angle."

"And how do you know that? How do you know anything I am capable of?"

"I've lived in fear of your shadow for the past five years. I've built my life around the obstacles you've thrown down. I read the letters my mother wrote to you for years. I know you, because I am so much like you even though I can't help it. You never do anything without trying to get something out of it for yourself. So, what was your aim today?"

"You flatter me, Aanya, but I must disappoint you."

"Again?"

"I have no ambitions left in me. No more goals to chase, no more angles to work. I was simply a lonely man in need of a little company tonight. And you gave it to me. You gave me more than I could have asked for. And such a show you put on too."

"A *show*? Is that what you think just happened here? A fucking show?!"

"Very entertaining if I don't say so myself. Quite a cast of characters too. An African, a Samoyed, two gypsies and a former Count. It's a shame all the playhouses are closed right now."

"You know what, Yoska?"

"What, Aanya?"

"Forget about what I said about not shooting my father. If it would make you happy, I think I'm just fine with it."

"Don't mind if I do. Heads up, Wilfred."

"No! Wait! Aanya, please! I'm your father!"

"And?"

"You don't really want to be responsible for killing me, do you?"

"I won't be killing you. Yoska will. And he's alright with it, aren't you, Yoska?"

"Yes. Perfectly fine with it."

"But, but…look at your poor mother."

"Don't you even *look* at her!"

"You don't want to lose both of your parents on the same day, do you?"

"I lost my parents when I was a child, Wilfred. I grew up an orphan in a gypsy camp. I made peace with losing you a long time ago. Even if I wasn't really all that sure what I was making peace with. Don't try to appeal to a piece of me I don't have."

"If you kill me, you won't ever be rid of…"

"Stop your groveling, Wilfred. It's embarrassing. Come on you guys, we're done here."

"NO! We're not done until *I* say we're done!"

5

The dinner party from hell was turning into a real-life inescapable nightmare. To make matters worse, a thunderstorm was raging overhead, as if to sympathize with the guests in the tumultuous early morning hours. The Red Army soldiers previously stationed outside all of the doors and windows were now positioned inside. And firmly so. There was nobody come in or out of this apartment until the sunrise shift change at the earliest. The rain was unrelenting outside so much so that just a little after midnight when the soldiers all came barreling in, the power went off. All of Petrograd seemed to be immersed in this painful, black, cloud of horror. There was no coping with this kind of hell. Jaina's body still lied on the dining room floor, a pile of drying red blood staining the hardwood around her face. Her mouth gaped open, eyes staring at anyone stupid enough to look at her. At one point Mila decided to pull the tablecloth off and cover the woman up, but Wilfred kept kicking and dragging it.

Dmitri's voice of reason, as quiet and subdued as it might have been, was a godsend when everyone in the cramped apartment needed some sort of direction. Everyone had a headache, was tired, and on edge. Yoska and Claude had their fingers wrapped around a trigger for hours. Mila had no more tears left in her body to cry, and Aanya was absolutely fuming at her father's amusement at all of this. Wilfred was too drunk to care about anybody being put out by this storm, or having to share the apartment overnight with a dead woman. The soldiers entertained themselves well enough, smoking in the kitchen and playing cards by candlelight. The front and back doors were barricaded with ten men a piece. There was not going to be some grand staged escape, to what? Run out into the torrential downpour? There was a leak in the roof, leaving a puddle in an upstairs bedroom that had begun to soak through the wallpaper of the ground floor. Flawless craftsmanship Dmitri had just paid for. Mila took a pot from the kitchen to try and assuage the situation, but there wasn't really any use. A leaky roof was the least of anyone's problems. Still, she was keeping herself busy as she only knew how to do, providing a service. When she took up a broom t begin sweeping, that's when Claude got a hold of her and locked the two in an upstairs bedroom to squabble through their own personal issues. They didn't do it very secretively. The dining room argument from hours earlier was only being renewed. It was awkward downstairs because Dmitri kept hearing his name shouted by Claude, and Aanya kept hearing her name shouted by Mila.

At around two in the morning the storm was beginning to make a river of the street out front. Leaning against the windows one could see the shine of the water in the as it rippled in the darkness. No street lights, only two brave souls on the streets had candles in their windows. Aanya's eyes had adjusted to the darkness by now, but she was still on pins and needles by the unfamiliarity of the apartment. This wasn't her home. It had never been. It would never be. She didn't know where the halls led, or where the rooms were. She didn't know what door would lead her to a safe space or not. Yoska shared in her desire to run from this place, and several times proposed a plan to do just that, but she never went along with it. Even if everyone was at each other's throats, no one was going to be left behind. Come sunrise, there would be more clarity, for everything. Time will have settled nerves, hopefully. She sat dejected on the pink velvet sofa, all curled up. Yoska had taken his brown patchwork jacket off and given it to her as a blanket. Dmitri could only watch, as he made himself the designated keeper of Wilfred's whereabouts, wherever that might have been. Usually, it revolved around the quickly emptying alcohol cabinet that was only ever restocked because the soldiers drained it as well as Wilfred. With all the anger pervading the apartment, Dmitri too indulged in a couple of glasses of vodka, much to Aanya's disapproval. But he didn't mind about upsetting her tonight. Her ire could be felt across the room until everyone jumped at the sound of a gun cocking into firing position. Wilfred had lost his mind, and was now on a shooting rampage downstairs.

Dmitri was the first to subdue the older man, but the struggle was difficult to navigate in the sheer darkness of the apartment. The storm continued to shake the house and drench the roof. Everyone was sent running this way and that, violently pushing and shoving each other into rooms and hallways. The soldiers upended the table, tripped over one another and secured the doors. Furniture was being tipped over as a shield. Yoska took evasive action at once and had Aanya by her shoulder, dragging her upstairs and out of harm's way while Wilfred descended into madness downstairs. The wrestling match was still taking place some five minutes later when Yoska found an unlocked bedroom and threw Aanya in ahead of him. He then went to work gathering and amassing all the possessions in the room up against the door. That was it. Dresser, nightstand, window side table, chair, and bedframe. The mattress had been removed for sleeping. Aanya sat on it alone while Yoska sat in front of her. Their knees touched as they sat cross legged, and their heads leaned into one another. This would not be a nostalgic repeat of their calm night down in Odessa last year. Yoska didn't have to even voice this out loud to see Aanya was already uncomfortable, clutching her flat stomach where their child had once grown. With his gun still loaded in his lap he clawed into the darkness for Aanya's hands. He could feel her nerves getting the best of her as she shook under her skin. Or maybe that was him. Or both of them. It was hard to tell. Everything was happening so intensely. They sighed together, and Yoska was able to see the white of Aanya's teeth light up in front of his face.

"There for a moment, I never thought I'd get to see such a beautiful sight as that smile of yours again."

"It's been a hell of a night, hasn't it, Yoska?"

"We've been through worse."

"Have we?"

"We'll get through this."

"All of us?"

"I'm not planning on losing anyone tonight."

"I don't think it matters what you have planned. I watched my mother die tonight, now it sounds like my father is desperate to join her."

"I know I'd lose my mind if I had to sit with your dead body for any amount of time. I can't blame the asshole for being suicidal now."

"You don't think I made a mistake earlier by stopping you from shooting him, do you?"

"It's hard to say what might have happened. But I was ready to do it for you had you let me. I still am ready, if you change your mind."

"Why?"

"Why what?"

"Why would you go so far for me? Why would you put up with all of this?"

"I'd do anything for you."

"But why?"

"I love you. What more reason does a man need to do anything?"

"I'm not worthy of such blind devotion."

"Who said I was blind in any of this? I'm fully aware of what's going on here. I see it all falling apart. I see you. I see me. I see us, together."

"I don't know that I see things the same way as you."

"We don't need to see things the same way."

"Thank you for getting me out of that room when you did. I think if I had been left to my own defense I would have just sat there and waited for a stray bullet to come and find me and take me away from it all."

"I know. When I threw myself onto the floor, I couldn't figure out why you were still sitting up by the window."

"I couldn't move. I knew what was happening, but I just couldn't get my body to react. It wasn't shock. But I don't know what it was."

"Sounds like shock to me."

"Have I become so weak in mind and character that I can't even control myself anymore?"

"It is not a weakness to be vulnerable."

"I lost control at the table earlier."

"You needed to."

"What do you mean?"

"You can't keep all of this anger inside of you and not expect it to leak out every now and then."

"I was wrong though to yell at Dmitri like I did."

"I think you were right on target."

"You would. I know how much you hate him."

"He doesn't deserve you."

"And you do?"

"No. Neither of us deserve you. You are a better woman than Dmitri and I combined. You are smarter, braver, wiser, more courageous, more beautiful…I could continue?"

"No. I get your point."

"Really? Because I don't think that you do. If you did, then I wouldn't still be able to feel you jump every time you heard Dmitri's voice."

"He needs help down there."

"He's in plenty good shape to handle Wilfred."

"But my father is deranged."

"And what's your solution? To go running down into the dark and try and get yourself caught up in all of that? Are you trying to get yourself shot?"

"I don't want anything to happen to Dmitri. Not before I got the chance to apologize to him."

"You've had hours to apologize since…"

BANG BANG

"AHH!"

"That was Dmitri, wasn't it?! Yoska, that was Dmitri! I have to help him! Help me move these things from the door. I have to get down there. Yoska! Yoska, help me! Help me!"

Aanya was tearing apart the furniture barricade like a wild animal. She was going to hurt herself if Yoska didn't jump up and push her out of the way. It was all he could do to pull the dresser back and crack the door open before she climbed up on the bedframe and squeezed and into the hallway. On the stairs she ran into Mila who'd heard the same scream from the former Count. Claude and Yoska were in no hurry going back downstairs where the soldiers were trying to make sense of the fight. Both Wilfred and Dmitri had blood on them because a collectible suit of armor from the corner of the room had toppled into their wrestling match on the floor. There were bits of armor strewn about, bloody noses, and the doors from the liquor cabinet pulled apart. Wilfred had shot Dmitri, who was now lying motionless on the ugly patterned rug. Aanya yelled for Wilfred to be removed from the room, and the old man was quickly drug by a dislocated arm and leg by the Red Army soldiers who didn't even question being commanded by a gypsy right now. As Mila and Aanya tried to assess where the blood was coming from and where the gunshot wound was, Dmitri was unresponsive. They were having trouble in the blackness of the room, and their emotions weren't helping any. Mila was a fit of tears again, and Claude was somehow able to make an exchange of secretly hidden rubles on his person for a candle. He came bearing light to Mila's side as Aanya tugged on his hand to canvas Dmitri's body. The bullet wound still couldn't be found. His clothes were so disheveled and torn, and hanging awkwardly on his limp body. Mila pulled away believing the worst when she saw the way Dmitri's limbs flopped as Aanya tried to lean him up on his side thinking the wound might have been on his back. Claude saw this too and knew Dmitri had to have been dead. He took the candle up towards

Yoska who realized Aanya was living in a suspended reality of her own creation right now and unwilling to accept the obvious truth. He bent down to the ground with her and tried to pull her away from the former Count's body but she just kept wrenching forwards out his hold each time. She became so angry with his interruptions that she actually shoved Yoska back on his hands and knees. That's where he decided she just needed some more time to process this, and stayed behind her, careful not to touch her, but remain close enough to catch her when she finally accepted the truth. Her hands were filtering over every inch of Dmitri's body, rifling through the folds of his pants, shirt, vest, and coat. Her fingers tumbled across a crinkle of paper in his breast pocket, and noticed it bore her name on it. She was confused, and Claude leaned in with the candle again. Aanya eyed Mila but the peasant shook her head in equal confusion. She'd never seen it before. It wasn't something Dmitri had made public, or carried routinely. If he had, it'd been a secret, just above his heart. Yoska saw the paper shaking in her hands as he sat behind her, and in an amazingly kind voice given the recent set of circumstances, he urged her to read the letter. She settled down on her heels as she unfolded the paper. It'd been folded so many times that the paper had been softened to a cloth like texture. It was written in Dmitri's fine hand. She caught herself laughing at how perfect his penmanship was, then noted the blurred blotches of ink where tears must have fallen while he wrote this. It was a poem, entitled, 'In Sunflower Fields'. Aanya's voice broke consistently as she read aloud.

"In Sunflower Fields, I first met you,
Outside the big cities, with skies so blue.
I didn't fit in, and you didn't care,
I built up my walls, while you danced bare.
The world seemed so small, if we only knew.

Now we're grown, that much is true,
We've laughed, we've cried, lost loved ones too.
But I'll never forget, the shine of your hair,
In Sunflower Fields.

And I dare not ask, for I have a clue,
That time's been less than kind towards you,
Regardless of that smile you wear.
But if you'd still like to run, I'll meet you there,
Where life is quiet and my heart is yours to lose,
In Sunflower Fields."

"That was a beautiful poem that he wrote for you, Aanya."

"It was, wasn't it, Mila?"

"I always saw him scribbling notes at his desk, but I never knew what he did with all of them. I thought he usually crumpled them up and threw them away. It appears this one escaped the trash bin."

"I am so thankful that it did."

"He's left you with kind words."

"That's still not good enough for me."

Aanya folded the letter up just like she had found it and put it back into Dmitri's breast pocket, tucking it into place like it still mattered. Then she took her hands to twist Dmitri's pale face back upwards towards the ceiling of the room, and ran her fingers through his sandy brown hair to get it sitting the way he liked it. She was doing a terrible job at stifling her sobs, but in the flickering light of the candle in Claude's hand, she could be seen smiling through the pain. She was delusional. The man was dead. He had to be. They had all heard the shot and subsequent scream. Mila fell into a crying spell once more. Claude and Yoska exchanged a brief mumbling of whispers before the candle was set down by Dmitri's side, and Claude took Mila back upstairs for the night. Yoska busied himself with cleaning up the surrounding area of debris, which included the gun Wilfred had been brandishing for hours. Aanya still fawned over Dmitri like he was merely sleeping. It was sad to watch so Yoska kept his back turned. As the minutes passed, he found sympathetic faces in each and every one of the Red Army soldiers. It's not like none of them hadn't seen a dead man before. But to see a dead man's woman so obsessed over his body, it was a painful look into the future at what the women in each of their own lives might do in a similar situation. Wives, girlfriends, mothers, sisters, aunts, and daughters. They couldn't even pick their card game back up again. Yoska covered Jaina's body again, punched Wilfred unconscious, and bummed a cigarette off of the commanding officer in charge for the night. Aanya meanwhile was hugging Dmitri as he laid on the ground, and she half on top of him. She was interlacing their fingers together and gripping his hand tight when she buried her face in his chest, and tried to accept the inevitable. But something was happening. The wind from the storm blew a chilly streak of air in through the cracks in the crooked front door, and sent shivers down Aanya's spine. She got goosebumps all over as she leaned up, hovering over Dmitri's body. She saw his neck too, was covered in goosebumps. She sucked in a gasp of air in happy confusion, and the felt Dmitri's fingers begin to tighten around her own. He wasn't dead! She threw her arms around his neck as he struggled upright to his side with Aanya's eager assistance. Yoska's cigarette dropped from his lips in disbelief and began burning a whole through the crotch of his pants, much to the delight of the soldiers sitting around him, equally as disturbed in the turn of events. Aanya was smothering Dmitri's face full of kisses as he laughed airily at the warm reaction. Then he rummaged through his shirt and jacket, and pulled out a sheet or the missing armor from the former eyesore in the room. It was dented severely from Wilfred's gunshot. The pain of the concussion had knocked the air out of the former Count's lungs and rendered him unconscious. He simply threw the plate aside now and pulled Aanya up into his lap, burying his face over her shoulder in a mass of her black hair.

"I never thought I'd be able to feel this happy again!"

"Thank you for waking up, Dmitri! Thank you, thank you, thank you!"

"You're welcome, Aanya."

"I'm so sorry for yelling at you earlier. You were right. I was angry and you didn't deserve what I…"

"I deserved everything you handed to me and then some. I'm sorry too."

"For what?"

"Not handling tonight better. I should have dealt with Wilfred weeks ago. When the Bolsheviks wanted to keep him here under house arrest, I should have just refused and paid them off. I'll fix this though. Come morning I'll ride straight for Moscow and get Wilfred out of here. I won't ever put you through something like this ever again."

"You better not! I don't ever want to think I've lost you, Dmitri. Not *ever* again!"

"I won't die on you, Aanya."

"You promise?"

"I love you too much to leave you. I'm a terribly selfish man, aren't I?"

"I love you *so* much, Dmitri."

"God, you have no idea how good it feels to hear you say that!"

6

Tuesday, 6th April

The Soviet Government under Lenin's control validated the Far East region of the country as a buffer zone to help keep the Japanese at bay. The move meant very little to the bulk of Russia which had been embroiled in war upon war in the western reaches. Today was not a calm one in Petrograd either. The forests had been swelling with gypsies, peasant, farmers, and factory workers now that the Spring thaw was in full swing. Today was still cold, with a bitter bite in the air, but the sun was overhead and the skies clean and blue. Before the sun was even up, it was apparent something was going down in Petrograd soon. The dirt paths and roads were full of angry voices descending upon the city center. They seemed to be responding to Green Army rumors trickling through the villages that a great protest was happening today. The Reds and Whites seemed surprised by the organization of local militia units and their renewing sense of hatred for the haves of the world. It had not died this past Winter at all.

On Aanya's command, and with Claude's support, the gypsy's own defense patrols were pulled in close to the tents to avoid being mixed up in the roving band of discontent flowing into Petrograd. Mila was kept safely tucked away in her tent because of the Far East decree. It'd been spoken for weeks now that the Japanese were testing the waters for another invasion. There were still many veterans of the Russian-Japanese War fifteen years ago to provide angst and discrimination to anyone of the Asian persuasion. No one was going to take any chances with Mila's safety after the year had already proven to be a deadly and turbulent one. One only had to look as far as the road to the hollowed ground of the former camp. With the recent regrowth of Spring at least the graves didn't look so mounded and obvious, and the blackened dirt from the fires of the Red Terror attack had softened back to a rich brown color. Jaina had been buried out there. After the deranged dinner party in February the group had brought the older gypsy woman's body back for proper mourning. It'd been a big deal, with a meager feast and a week's worth of celebrations in honor of the contested woman. Wilfred didn't have any say in the matter since he'd been moved by the Red Army soldiers to another location on the Nevsky Prospekt for house arrest. The Bolsheviks had many enemies, and Wilfred was going to be dealt with accordingly when his day of reckoning came, which wasn't going to be anytime soon. Aanya had no intention of visiting her father anymore or being informed of where his new address was, but Dmitri had been sent a telegram from the buyer of his apartment in good faith. He burned the strip of paper without reading it to maintain a clear head, and Aanya approved of that gesture. His support meant everything to her, and since she'd almost lost him in February the two had been on the best of terms, like when they were kids. Yoska popped in less and less to the camp as the weeks had passed, but with the surge of activity today, and the Green Army to blame, he did invite himself into the group's close quarters and extend a hand out to them to join the protests. Claude refused on the basis of Mila's safety, but Dmitri was a quiet observer. He'd let Aanya decide for him, as he didn't care to participate or not. Yoska was somewhat hopeful now, and had a gleam in his big brown eyes as he looked down to his favorite person in the whole world.

"Just what are you getting at with this protest today, Yoska? What do the Greens think they're going to get done that hasn't been done by storming the city before?"

"We're going after the aristocrats today."

"What do you mean going after them?"

"Word has it that they've come back into the cities. They've been hiding in the country the past two years but a lot of them have returned to their old ways. The Bolsheviks are supporting a new, political high society. We want to stop that before it gets started. So, Aanya, can I count on you to come with me?"

"Dmitri might know some of these people."

"It's alright, Aanya. I have no love loss for a majority
of my former peers. Anyone I was on good terms
with has fled to France, England, and the United
States."

"They have?"

"Yes. That's what most of my telegrams have been
for. They've been leaving since 1917. I just wasn't in
the position or frame of mind to follow them then.
They asked. Believe me, they pushed for me to join
them, but I had other important matters on my mind."

"Me?"

"I could never leave Russia without you, Aanya."

"Would you leave with me?"

"I'd buy the tickets right now if you wanted me to."

"If we helped Yoska clean the town up though,
maybe we wouldn't have to take such drastic
measures as leaving our home?"

"You're unusually optimistic about the current
political climate. Might I ask why?"

"Yoska is a persuasive man, don't you think?"

"We've differing opinions when it comes to Yoska."

"Yoska is still standing right here, just so you two lovebirds know."

"I'm sorry, Yoska. I didn't mean to be talking around you. It's just, I know I can be a little soft when it comes to your reasoning. I was hoping Dmitri might be able to keep me in line."

"He said he'll go with whatever you decide, Aanya. So, all that I'm waiting for is for you to say yes to me."

"If I say yes, what exactly am I saying yes too? Because I can run into the streets and protest, but I can't burn shopkeepers' front doors, and break their windows, and steal from the marketplace. I can't hurt the poor to punish the rich."

"This isn't going to be like the protests two years ago. I promise. This is going to be different."

"It looks like the same people. Why are they any different than they were two years ago?"

"Because I've got a hand at leading them now."

"You hold rank with the Greens?"

"Informally."

"I'm so proud of you, Yoska!"

"I was hoping you would be."

"Then Dmitri and I will follow you into the city. Maybe we can make a change where the last riots were unable to do so. Stop the problem before it gets started. That's a cause I can get behind."

"Great! Then we need to run and catch up to the front of the crowds if we want to make a real difference in the city today. Can I ask you for one more favor, Aanya?"

"Sure."

"Might I be lucky enough to borrow some of your horses?"

"How many?"

"Ten?"

"I'll get them and meet you at your camp as fast as I can. How does that sound?"

"Music to my ears. I knew I could count on you!"

Yoska's face had never looked so happy. Dmitri was quiet this whole time as he saw the gypsy man's face mimicked in Aanya's. That friendship, that close bond those two had, Dmitri was never going to get rid of that. He'd have to learn to live with it. It was more about swallowing his pride than anything else. He wasn't going to share the love of his life, but he was going to have to accept that other people were important to her aside from just him. She still wore his silver key bracelet on the rotten green ribbon. She still slept by his side every night, and spent most of the day within an arm's reach of him. She was his, body and soul, but Yoska wasn't going anywhere. Whenever he came to Aanya, she lights up. She listens intently. And he knows that. He knows he can get just about anything he asks for, whether he deserves it or not. One day Dmitri might have to put his foot down, draw a line in the sand or something of that nature, but today was not that day. Today was about bonding together for the common good. Eliminating the haves from having so much and have nots from having nothing. Dmitri was officially without his countship as of his divorce. He still had a sizeable chunk of wealth, but it was hidden for safe keeping. He was an everyday man once more. No fine suits and grand parties. He was nervous coming into this protest, but with Aanya by his side he was able to leech off of some of her confidence. On horseback the leaders of the Green Army stormed through the streets of Petrograd with ferocity unmatched by previous demonstrations. Thousands of voices were making themselves heard.

One vein of the protest made its way to the Nevsky Prospekt. Chants and sit-ins were already in full swing by the time Dmitri and Aanya ran down the thoroughfare on foot. Some of the most important people and shops were here. Grand buildings painted every color of the rainbow, with fancy trim and lush interiors, overworked walls and overindulgent patrons. The rich cowered behind the windows. The violence was negligible today, but the police still didn't stand a chance at maintaining order. They were overwhelmed, swamped by the sheer numbers pooling into the city squares and public spaces. Red Army soldiers which had been standing guard at private residences had been called upon to aid the meager police force in their attempt to regain control of the city. This left Wilfred and a handful of other Bolshevik enemies vulnerable under house arrest. The German Prinz was detoxing off of alcohol and imported opium from the Orient. He was in a bad way, sour at the world, and sore at life. He'd come down with a terrible case of the flu last month and still had yet to get over the dizzy spells, nausea, and troubling cough. As a result of his sickness, thought by some of the sponsored doctors to be none other than the Spanish Flu which had gripped the world the last year or so, Wilfred had been kept in isolation. No social interaction whatsoever. The man was full mad. With people surging in the streets, he wanted desperately to be apart of something. He came out his unguarded front door wrapped in a black robe, fur lined, with fancy slippers. Even in decay, he still looked the part of arrogantly rich former self. Wilfred was identified almost immediately after he got tumbled into the younger protesting public, and tossed back and forth from one unsympathetic marcher to another. A small pit of anger seemed to be congregating around himself as he spoke in defense of his name. After being scoffed at he was punched, and then punched again, and again, until finally he fell to his knees and was kicked to the ground. Wilfred was beaten by an angry mob of Greens, and Aanya stood ten feet away, silent.

"Aanya, Aanya let's get out of here."

"No. Not yet, Dmitri."

"What are you waiting for?"

"I want to know that man is dead before I turn my back on him."

"Why?"

"I want to see if he understands why this is happening. I want to know his end was nothing more special than getting beaten and left for dead no different than a piece of trash."

"I'm sure he knows."

"Let me have this."

"Why do you *need* this?"

"For abandoning my mother, *twice*. For not being any part of my life or Gyorgi's. He chose Lotte over my family. And I can't even be angry with Lotte anymore. I can only be angry with him. These were the choices he made in his life and they all went from bad to worse. He tried to cheat every system he came across. But he couldn't cheat them all. He can't cheat me anymore. He's done. I need to see him draw his last breath. I need that closure."

"Aanya?"

"What?"

"Did you know Wilfred was being held on house arrest on this street?"

"Yes."

"How?"

"Yoska told me."

"How did he know?"

"I didn't care to ask. He has his own set of resources. And I am thankful to him."

"You knew that I knew about Wilfred, and didn't tell you, didn't you?"

"I assumed you had your reasons. I'm not angry with you for lying to me about my father. I figured you were doing it for my own good. You were only keeping it from me for my own good, right?"

"I have no reason to lie to you unless it's in an effort to keep you safe or sane. But if I may…"

"Hold on. The people are moving. I can see him now. He's almost…dead."

"Good. Now you have your closure."

"Let me stand here for a moment, please?"

"A dead man does not become deader the longer you stare at him."

"My brother never got to know who his father was, Dmitri. My mother killed herself to escape this man, this man right here in front of me. My sister, be it half blooded or full blooded makes no difference to me. Lotte died to escape this man. You left your entire world behind, your title, marriage, status, because of this man."

"I'd leave it all again in the hopes you winning you."

"Then for me, just be patient right now."

"I am being patient. But every man has his limits."

"Why do I have the feeling you're referring to something more than my father and my need to see him dead?"

"You never told me you've been meeting Yoska in secret to get information about your father."

"I knew it'd only upset you."

"When have you even been doing this? The only time we spend any time apart is when I go get firewood."

"You are gone for an hour at least. It's all the time I needed."

"Why can't I be enough for you?"

"You are enough for me, Dmitri."

"But you still hang on his every word."

"I hang on yours as well."

"I don't want to be jealous of him but you're not giving me much of a choice in the matter. As long as he remains a constant figure in your life, I will always be questioning my place in your heart."

"I don't want you to question anything."

"But I am."

"What do you want me to do to make that up to you?"

"I can't ask you what I want."

"I know what you can't say."

"Then why did you ask me to say it?"

"To hear how ridiculous, it sounds."

"Why is it ridiculous?"

"Yoska was there for me when you left me. He's always been ready to help me and support me whenever the moment called. You haven't."

"You won't ever sever your ties to him?"

"I can't, and I won't."

"I dropped everything I had for you though."

"I didn't ask you to leave any of your world behind. If you miss it, I won't stop you from rejoining it."

"You won't?"

"I won't ever stand in the way of what you want. I just foolishly thought I was at the top of that list again. But I guess we can't ever reach that high we had when we were sixteen, huh?"

"We can, if we fight for it."

"We didn't fight when we were sixteen. That was the beauty of what we had. It was effortless. It was easy, and it was safe."

"You remember how I was talking about all of my friends leaving Russia, back at camp?"

"Yes. You've brought it up multiple times, as have Claude, Mila, Yoska, Jaina…"

"What do you think about it?"

"I think what I have always thought. Running from Russia doesn't mean our life will just magically become hassle free."

"But would you be open to giving it a try?"

"Now?"

"If not right now, very soon?"

"I don't want to leave the only home I've ever known. I know Petrograd is full of problems, but they're my problems. These are my streets. That's my forest out there. These are my people."

"You can set down new roots and start a fresh life somewhere else. Anywhere else."

"You speak as if you still have all the money in the world at your fingertips."

"What if I told you that I did?"

"What are you talking about? I thought between my father and the divorce that you'd lost it all?"

"I am smarter than everyone thinks I am. I have enough money for a new life, if you'd only take my hand and join me."

"I'm scared."

"I'd be right there with you every step of the way. I don't need your answer right now. Just promise me that you'll think about it?"

"I promise."

7

Monday, 2nd August

The Green Army ranks have grown to the tune of some forty thousand people. With neither Red nor White support, they have persisted to be a thorn in the sides of the establishment. The Bolsheviks might be on the verge of a breakthrough though to completely crush the spirit of the people they formally championed as the most important resource in all of Russia. An aggressive grain tax has been lobbied against the poor, peasant, and farming communities resulting in the Tambov Uprising. The Greens will not be forced to pay for the Reds control of the country. Riots from town to town are spreading like wildfire that cannot be quenched. But the Bolsheviks are trying. They still have the greatest amount of resources and people at their disposal. The Red Terror that's been in place since the revolution has not been extinguished. Brutal tactics when necessary are being employed to silence whoever speaks out. Summer has turned into a nightmare with no end in sight. Russia simply can't go on like this.

Saturday, 14th August

The Vistula River in Poland, the largest river in the region, has just experienced a miracle today. A Green Army hotspot in the huge population center of Warsaw has been protected in what's being called an act of God. Red Army troops had been deployed to take the city by force, but somehow the people managed to protect themselves in such staggering circumstances that the Bolsheviks actually had to pull themselves back for fear of public embarrassment. The damage is already done though. Once word spreads of Warsaw's victory, more towns will band together to make the defeat a common occurrence rather than a mere fluke. There is real optimism now that the tides might be turning in the people's favor after all, that all their struggles over the past five years have not been in vain. One can hope when hope is all that many people have been left with in this world. Livelihoods have been decimated; families destroyed. Territories have changed so many hands so many times that it's hard to keep track of it all, but still people push on, and move forward. In the Green Army outpost just outside of Aanya's camp in Petrograd, there were grand celebrations to be heard that evening. Progress had been made. Real progress. Tangible progress. Yoska couldn't resist coming over to the gypsies to share the good news. Aanya and Mila were elbows deep in ladling out soup though, so Yoska had to settle for conversation with Dmitri and Claude who were eager for political discourse, but not so much for Yoska's company. Beggars couldn't be choosers though, so they engaged in discussion while Aanya happily looked on at all the important men in her life being civil with one another. She playfully nudged Mila beside her to take note of the progress being made. Real progress. Tangible progress. Had she heard the men speaking though, and looked harder at their faces, she might not have been so excited. Claude was standoffish and hesitant to match Yoska's level of enthusiasm while Dmitri put on a good face but let the pitch of his voice fall into an obviously disinterested monotone.

"Easy, Yoska. Breathe man. What is this Miracle on the Vistula you're rambling about?"

"Claude, I have to hand it to the French. They really supported the Greens out there in Warsaw today."

"It is good to know the French have no abandoned us out here. I'd like to think I might be welcomed back home one of these days."

"Are you guys still entertaining that idea that Russia is a lost cause?"

"Claude and I are only thinking realistically, Yoska. We have our women and our futures to think about. Please don't take this offense personally."

"How could I not take this personally? You want to take Aanya away from me."

"I'm not taking Aanya anywhere she doesn't want to go. So, just calm down."

"When are you going to understand that she doesn't want to leave, Dmitri?"

"When I am able to understand that it is Russia she doesn't want to leave behind, instead of you, then I will be satisfied with her reluctance to follow me where I can provide a good life for her."

"If you're so confident in your ability to provide for her, then you'd be able to give her the life she deserves in the home she's most comfortable in. And that's right here."

"She's still confused."

"She's not confused. You're just unwilling to admit to me how important I am in her life."

"I'm not unwilling to admit that. But she is using you as an excuse. You are a crutch for her. You are familiar. And you're holding her back."

"That's a bold accusation, Dmitri."

"I mean every word, Yoska."

"How am I holding her back? She's happy here. She's with her people. Look at her smiling over there. What more could she want in life?"

"Peace. Stability. I could list a million things she wants but is too humble and modest to ask for."

"You're not the only man in the world who knows her, you know."

"I do know. But unlike you, I can give her a life worth living. You can't."

"You still sitting on a wad of cash somewhere that nobody knows about?"

"Aanya knows I have money. I've told her about all of our possibilities. And Claude supports me too when it comes to leaving Russia. Mila would follow this man anywhere. The only sticking point in all of our potential happiness is you."

"You can't blame everything that goes wrong in life on me."

"No, but a lot of it does circle back around to you eventually."

"Name one thing I'm responsible for."

"You were sneaking around talking to Aanya behind my back."

"So? That was her choice. I owe my loyalty to *her*, not *you*. It wasn't my idea to keep you in the dark."

"It wasn't?"

"No. It was hers. I didn't want to sneak around like a teenager again, but that's what she wanted, so I gave it to her. She knows anytime she even brings me up around you that you get upset. And I'm a big enough man to recognize how much she loves you."

"You're a big enough man to say it, but not a big enough man to accept it."

"You can't accept it either."

"I can accept that Aanya loves me."

"But you can't accept that she loves me too."

"She doesn't love us the same."

"Now that, I will agree with you on, and that may be the only thing."

"Why did you come here tonight?"

"To tell Aanya my good news."

"And why do you think she would have cared about something that happened in Warsaw?"

"Because it made me happy."

"And her happiness hinges on your own?"

"She is supportive of me."

"Can you say the same?"

"Yes."

"If Aanya wanted to leave Russia, you'd support her?"

"Yes. But she doesn't want to leave Russia, *you* do. And she doesn't want what you want."

"We want a life together."

"Then have it. But do it here."

"We can't have a life worth living in Russia. We're just going from one war to the next. That's no place to raise a family."

"You two are talking about that?"

"We have multiple times. Why? Does that upset you, Yoska?"

"You've spoken about having children?"

"We want a family together, so yes, that involves her having my children."

"And she's alright with that?"

"Yes! Why are you having so much trouble understanding what I'm trying to say?!"

"She never told you what happened, did she?"

"What happened when?"

"It's not my place to say. That's up to her to tell you if she chooses."

"What are you even talking about?"

"I just told you, it's not my place to say. What happened was between her and I, but it took a much greater toll on her, understandably."

"Did something happen to Aanya?"

"It was a while ago now. Over a year."

"I'd still like to know."

"Then you need to speak with Aanya. I wouldn't betray her trust like that."

"This was something serious, wasn't it?

"Life altering, I'd say."

"And you didn't like the outcome, did you, Yoska?"

"No. Not at all. But it wasn't her fault. It wasn't anybody's fault. Some things just happen, and no one can explain it. Do I wish I could have changed what happened? Yes. Every damned day. But I couldn't then, and I can't now. It was what it was. Bad timing. Story of my life."

"Are you alright, Yoska?"

"What do you care, Claude?"

"I don't care. But for Aanya's sake, please do your best to put on a smile, she's been watching us like a hawk the entire time you've been here and I don't want to get lectured again about us not being nice to you."

"She lectures you guys on being nice to me?"

"Every time you come around."

"She's a good woman. You know what, Dmitri? I'm going to step back right now. I'm going back to my camp. You have some things you need to handle, and I do too. I'm going to go. I'll put a smile on for Aanya, but that's about the best I can do right now. Will you guys excuse me?"

No sooner did Yoska leave did Aanya's smile fade from her blood red stained lips. She excused herself from soup duty and handed her ladle off to the gypsy woman beside her, a young little thing of about seventeen and eager to please. Claude made himself scarce in a hurry too, going over to Mila's concerned side to give her a quick briefing of what had just been discussed. Dmitri looked to his former servant's face for any clues of what was going on, but he received no comfort. Aanya was upset, and gripped Dmitri firmly by his forearm to drag him to the confines and privacy of their shared tent. But once they were alone it was apparent that she no longer held the authority that she did when all the camp's eyes were on her. Out there she was a leader, in here, she was merely half of a whole, and her other half was just as upset as she was. Initially she was going to grill Dmitri at pushing Yoska way before she got the chance to see him and share in his good news. But now, seeing Yoska go from excited to ejected in such a hurry, and to see Dmitri share in that dejection, she was cautious about how to approach this awkward situation. Dmitri was biting his bottom lip again, and not fond of holding eye contact. It got so bad that Aanya found herself lurching down to try and see eye to eye with him, like something little Ruslo might do when she was upset in the forest. Only with her fox she could giggle, and this, whatever it was now, it was no laughing matter. Not even close. When she reached out to take Dmitri's hand he pulled back, and shook his head no. She recoiled like she'd just been bitten, and her anger was able to restore her confidence.

"What's wrong now, Dmitri? I will not sit here and be scolded when I don't even know what it is you're trying to punish me for."

"Yoska brought something to my attention."

"And?"

"He had a hard time accepting the fact that we were going to start a family."

"Well, one day, I hope. But you didn't give him the impression that I was pregnant right now, did you?"

"No. I'm sorry, do I need to stop talking so you can go run out and see if he's alright?"

"I don't appreciate your sarcasm."

"And I don't appreciate you lying to me."

"What do you think I've been lying to you about?"

"He said something happened to you last year. Something he wasn't happy about. What is he talking about, Aanya?"

"That's too vague for me to elaborate on. You're going to have to be more specific. A lot of things happened last year."

"Don't play games with me. You know what I'm talking about, don't you?"

"Yoska didn't say what happened?"

"He said it wasn't his place. Only that you told him to keep it between the two of you."

"He's a man of his word. You have to respect that."

"Aanya, why would us starting a family together upset him so much? This was more than just a man being jealous."

"He's probably just worried about me, that's all."

"Why does he have to be worried about you?"

"I…"

"You can tell me anything, Aanya."

"You won't like what I have to say. It's not something I'm proud of. I haven't told anyone this. I didn't even tell Yoska. He just found me."

"Found you?"

"In the sunflower fields. *Our* sunflower fields. That was a beautiful poem you wrote me."

"You read it?"

"Back in the apartment. I thought you had died on me. I found it and read it. I'm sorry."

"Don't be. I'm glad you liked it. But don't get side tracked. What happened in the sunflower fields?"

"I…I…"

"Aanya? Come on, it's really alright."

"Forgive me, if I want to remember what your face looks like right now, before I break you."

"*Break* me? Aanya there's nothing you could possibly say that would ever make me think any less of you. Nothing, alright? You say you aren't proud of what happened, that's fine. Don't be proud."

"It's one of the worst things to ever happen to me."

"I will love you no matter what, Aanya. I will love you in your darkness. I don't care."

"You wouldn't care that I lost Yoska's baby?"

"You…"

"I told you that I'd break you!"

"Easy, easy now. I'm not broken."

"I was about half way through my pregnancy. I felt something wrong. I got these sharp pains. I hadn't told anyone. I wasn't even showing that much. That should have been my first clue that something wasn't right. But I didn't know what to do. I was so scared. I just ran for the fields. I didn't know where else to go. He found me out there, Yoska did. I don't even know how. But he saw what happened. I had to tell him that it was his. I lost his baby. He deserved to know that I had failed him."

"I'm so sorry that happened to you. No wonder he was so upset when he left."

"He knows how upset I was that day. The truth is, I was ready to be a mother. I've wanted it for years. But after what happened, I don't know if that's something I'm ever going to be able to experience or not. And if I can't have children, then…I don't know where that might put you and me?"

"You think I would leave you if I knew you couldn't give me a child?"

"You divorced Lotte for that."

"No. I mean, legally on paper it was a good argument, but I divorced Lotte because I never wanted to marry her in the first place, because I never loved her. I love you, Aanya."

"But having children is like the one thing a woman is supposed to accomplish in life. If I can't even do that, what good am I?"

"You are no less of a woman in my eyes, you understand me?"

"There's a very real possibility that I'll never be able to give you the life you want. So, you keep coming down on me, asking me to leave Russia. I keep saying no. That's one of my biggest reasons, Dmitri. I don't want to let you down after you go through all the hassle of getting us out to this fresh new life of ours, only to find out I can't give you anything you ask for in return. I could never live with myself if I knew I disappointed you."

8

The longer the struggle, the more people come out to fight. In Ukraine there has been a new force pushing for rights amongst a broken Russian transition of power. Now the Black Army, a group of anarchist guerilla fighters, are pushing in line with the Red Army to stop, or at the very least slow, the inward advance of the White and Green Armies on the rich farmland regions of the south. It is the Black and the Reds opinion to rebuild the economy on the backs of grain producers. And with a rebuilt economy, everything else will just somehow fall into place. Problems will vanish into thin air. There aren't real solutions or real answers anymore. Absolutely every aspect of life has been politicized. Two weeks ago, Yoska came asking Aanya for help in the Ukraine region, knowing something wrong was taking place. Like a trusting fool, Aanya agreed. Half the gypsies willing to fight traveled down south with Aanya and Dmitri, while Yoska led the Green Army. Claude and Mila had been left in the camp in

Petrograd to maintain stability and order, but with this news breaking this afternoon, tensions soared. Claude couldn't ever handle the pressure and anxieties of people in pain. He caved with them. He was too sympathetic for his own good, too soft for such a hard exterior that he prided himself on portraying. Mila knew the real toll this news was taking on her man though, and knew that his desire was, and had been for two weeks now, to be hands on in Ukraine. When he came into their tent today for reassurance that he was doing the right thing in staying here, he saw her packing his bag for him. But she was not packing one for herself. Her eyes were wet with tears, but she smiled as he held her face in his hands.

"I am so confused right now, Mila."

"I know you are. But I'm not."

"Good. Then tell me what to do and I'll do it. I'll listen to anything you have to say. I just need an order to follow."

"Go to Ukraine with the others."

"Are you sure?"

"It's where your head has been ever since they left. You stayed behind for me, and for the camp, but you do not owe us anything."

"I don't want to upset you if I leave though."

"You've upset me enough already by acting against your own free will. I do not want to be responsible for a regret in your life. You and Dmitri talk all the time about how Yoska holds Aanya back. I don't want anyone to see the same mistake being made between you and I."

"You are nothing like, Yoska. Absolutely nothing."

"Thank you, but I *am* holding you back."

"What if you were to come with me?!"

"No. I can't. It's too dangerous."

"I'll protect you."

"Don't bring me with you, Claude. I'll only get everyone killed. I don't belong on the front lines; I belong on the home front. That is my place in life. It always has been. And I am not ashamed of it. There are fighters, and there are the people who support the fighters. I don't mind being your support system. But as far as this is concerned, I will support you from a distance."

"I will miss you."

"I will miss you too. But you will be back soon enough. I don't think that the Whites and the Greens have what it'll take to stop the Blacks and the Reds from doing whatever they want."

"Russia has become a lost cause, hasn't it?"

"People have been saying it for months."

"But do you believe it now?"

"What does it matter if a little nobody like me from Siberia thinks her home country has fallen to pieces?"

"You're not just a little nobody to me. You're everything. And I'm going to marry you."

"You are?"

"I had hoped when it came around time to asking you, I would have done something more special than this. But I want you to understand how important you are to me. I want to marry you, Mila."

"I want to marry you too, Claude!"

"Then I'll take it up with Aanya as soon as I see her."

"I guess I'm going to have to get used to be called your wife then, won't I?"

"I think it has a nice ring to it. You look like a good wife to me."

"And then we'll have children?"

"As many as we can!"

"Here?"

"It doesn't matter where we'll be, so long as we're together. And we will be. This is the last time I'm going to walk away from you. I promise. No more fighting for me."

"You be careful out there."

"I will be. I'm going to make sure Aanya and Dmitri come home. I won't come back without them."

"How long do you think you'll be gone?"

"A week probably. I don't know how difficult it will be to navigate the roads. But with my French uniform on, I might make pretty good time."

"You're not just being overly optimistic for my benefit, are you?"

"I would never lie to you, Mila."

"Then I wish you good luck. And I'll see you soon."

"Please don't cry."

"Oh, don't worry about that. These are happy tears! I promise."

"Happy tears?"

"The happiest. I'm going to be your wife!"

Mila laughed as she cried, and Claude knew he had made the right decision in proposing to her. Maybe he could have been a little more formal in the whole matter, but the sentiment was there. She was glowing with excitement. Her rosy round cheeks were fully blushed as the tears streamed down. But she quick to wipe them away as she tucked Claude's pack around his shoulder. Then she kept her fingers busy with buttoning his blue jacket, and making sure it sat squarely on his shoulders. She outlined his frame with her hands, slowly, making sure to memorize it for the days to come. He would come home soon. He had to. She knew this to be true. She knew it as certain as she knew the sun would rise in the morning and set at night. She was going to be just fine. Mila laughed off her tears again as Claude kissed her softly and hopped onto his black horse. When she waved goodbye there was small talk in pockets around the camp that something had gone wrong down in Ukraine. Claude was leaving because Aanya and Dmitri were in trouble. Mila wasn't strong enough to maintain the camp on her own. She was no leader; she was just another helping hand. Many of the strongest personalities were gone too. Yoska's men, the fighters, the veterans. It was mainly just women and children here, a handful of the elderly and a group of the sick off to the side. Everyone had to take care of themselves. Some of the gypsies from the Moscow band who'd spent months here took this as a sign to finally go back home and take their chances in more familiar grounds. Others were thinking of doing the same. If the Reds really were ending this war, then it was time to go home.

Claude would make excellent time on his travels south, but until he reached the Ukraine, the Greens and the gypsies were still in the thick of the fight. The Whites cared little for their militia support and unorganized troops. Everyone was segregated in the south. The Blacks, who initially like the Greens had hated both of the established forms of government, had sold themselves out to the Reds. There were any number of reasons for that move. They could have just realized that their guerilla tactics were not going to be successful in the long term, or they'd be paid a hefty amount of rubles and promised ridiculous amounts of security in exchange for their silence. Whatever the case, there was no longer a glimmer of hope that the Bolsheviks were going to be taken down. This four-year civil war was going to prove no more fruitful than the four-year Great War had. Russia's people had all been made orphans. There was no work to be had, no livable wage, no ample food supply. It had brought out the worst in humanity. Brothers selling out their fellow brother. It was despicable behavior. There was not going to be any return to normal. The calm before the storm would never be resumed. To make matters worse tonight was left without a shred of moonlight, and maneuvers were on the rise. It was incredibly uneasy in one's own skin, and gunfire kept popping off every few minutes, with the sporadic round of artillery fire to keep things interesting. There would be no sleeping in the weeks of preparation. Exhaustion was as rampant as desperation. Suicides could be found at the bottom of every bridge and canyon. A shot to the head was among the most popular forms of death as Aanya soon found. She'd see a man sloped over to his side, and rush to his aide only to find he'd wandered off hours ago to die. There was nothing Dmitri or Yoska could do to slow her down. It was almost as if she wanted to bury her pain in the pain of others. Neither of them had ever seen her on the front lines before. It was a far cry from the lengths she was willing to go to in the normal day to day life. She was the bloodiest, despite not brandishing a gun, and she was the least skittish, despite constantly running in front of everyone. There was a wife of one of the older men leading the Green Army who'd been doing nursing work all day who finally called out to Aanya for an extra pair of hands as she struggled to carry out surgical removals of bullets by candlelight. Aanya jumped at the distraction while Dmitri and Yoska followed side by side much further behind, careful to keep an eye on their woman. They were reluctantly comrades now, sharing what remained of a canteen, and leaning up against the base of a tree for support. Neither man could take their eyes off of Aanya, her flawless shadow and her lack of hesitation to get wrist deep into a man's abdomen.

"I don't know how she does it, Yoska."

"I don't know either. But she's good at it, isn't she?"

"She's good at everything she does. That woman doesn't know how to let people down."

"She's going to run herself to death soon."

"No. We'll stop her before she goes that far."

"*We?*"

"This is the way she wants it. Both of us by her side. I'll do whatever I can to keep that pretty smile of hers on her face."

"I've been thinking about that."

"Thinking about what?"

"I can't just pretend to be alright with the fact that you won, Dmitri. I can't do it. I want to keep her happy too, but not if it keeps killing me inside. There comes a time when a man has to back down and save face."

"Is this you backing down?"

"Yes, I think it is. I don't want this life for her. I don't like seeing her this manic. She's got blood all over her and it's like she doesn't even care. There's no enjoyment in that. No pleasure. You say you can give her a good life?"

"I know I can."

"Far away from here I hope."

"I've been talking to my friends overseas."

"Does she know?"

"I don't think so. If she does, she's playing ignorant really well."

"It's a done deal then?"

"In a couple months she could be removed from all of this."

"She'll be happy with you. She might miss Russia at first, but once she sees that everything you've promised her can be real, I think she'll be just fine."

"She told me about what happened last year, Yoska, and why she's really afraid to leave."

"So, you *did* manage to pull it out of her?"

"I'm sorry for your loss. Truly, I am."

"Like I said before, maybe it wasn't the right time for Aanya and I to have a child together. I wouldn't want to raise a kid up in all of this hell. It just wouldn't be right."

"She's worried she can't have children."

"She's got a right to worry. That doesn't bother you, does it?"

"As much as I'd love to have that perfect family with kids running all around the yard, as long as I had her and she was happy, I know I could be happy too."

"You're a good man, Dmitri."

"Thank you. You know, you might not be all that bad yourself, Yoska."

"I wish it didn't have to be like this."

"I do too."

"I'm going to miss her so much."

"Well, whenever we get settled, you're more than welcome to come out and visit us. I'll pay for your ticket expenses and everything. So, don't worry about that."

"And just how do you expect to get word back to me?"

"I assumed you'd go back up to the camp in Petrograd, and take over there."

"I don't know if I could handle being there without her. I might just pick up my things and start fresh for myself somewhere else."

"I wish you nothing but the best, whatever you decide. But I know it would make Aanya happy if she knew that she wasn't walking away from you forever."

"She's a strong woman. She'll manage."

"But will *you* manage?"

"We hate each other, Dmitri. I don't need you to pretend to care about me now."

"We don't really hate each other though, do we?"

"You got my girl. I *should* hate you for besting me at something as important as winning over Aanya. But I can't."

"When we leave, I'll be sure to leave a little something behind for you."

"I don't want your money, Dmitri."

"It will make me feel better to know you won't be in such dire straits."

"It's pity money, and I'd burn it to keep myself warm before I spent it for pleasure."

"Will you take anything from me?"

"No. Nothing will make up for taking Aanya away. But this is the way it must be. She might not be thrilled at first, but I won't let her stay here. I won't have it. I won't have any more of this. Jaina told me that Aanya will lead a fulfilling life. And she didn't see me in it, but she never could see me. I don't know what that means, but I have to believe that Aanya will be better for our parting sooner rather than later."

"It takes a good man to accept defeat."

"Don't go calling me a good man, Dmitri. It will ruin my reputation. And if a man doesn't have his reputation, what does he have?"

"Friends?"

"Friends in foreign countries don't count if you never see them. And we will never see each other once you leave. You may have grand hopes of writing letters and sending telegrams but we both know what's going to happen. You and Aanya will move on together, and I will be left behind here, to fight it out in whatever remains of mother Russia."

"You're a good fighter though."

"I am, aren't I?"

"Instinctually good. That's got to be something worth being proud of, isn't it?"

"I'd rather have Aanya."

"But we can't both have her."

"I know. But in my dreams, I have her. You won't ever be able to take those away from me."

"When we do leave, can you do me a favor, Yoska?"

"That depends on the favor."

"Don't let her know that when you're saying goodbye, that it'll be forever. Let her hold onto the hope that she'll see you again."

"You want me to lie to her?"

"She's already going to be broken. Do you really want to ruin her?"

"I'll think of something. You will give me a couple of days warning though, won't you? So, I can at last try and get my words together?"

"I'll keep you informed. But plan on it being around the holidays. I want to give the tickets to her as a present."

"Well, that'd be a much better present than what I gave her two years ago when Gyorgi died. I guess tickets to a new future trumps a dead brother, now doesn't it?"

"You have a dark sense of humor, Yoska."

"I have to try and laugh about something or I'm going to wind up no better than all these guys we ran across tonight. Sitting here freezing with a bullet in my head."

"I won't let you kill yourself."

"I won't let you stop me."

9

Sunday, 7th November

There was chaos in the Crimean Peninsula today, on what is being celebrated as the third-year anniversary of the Bolshevik takeover of Russia. The Reds forced the surrender of the Whites at the seaside city of Perekop. Adverse weather in the form of subzero temperatures, and gale force winds wasn't helping matters any, and what was supposed to be a battle turned into more of a one-sided slaughter and botched evacuation attempt. While the Reds with their new Black Army support suffered a staggering ten thousand deaths and one hundred and nineteen thousand casualties, the Whites took on two thousand deaths and forty-one thousand casualties. The key to understanding the hurt the White and Greens felt today though was in the percentages. The Blacks and Reds just ha so many people at their disposal that even losing as many as they did dint' seem to slow them down at all, whereas the Whites and the Greens lost sometimes ninety percent of their factions. There was no leg for them to stand on anymore. There would be no return to the Imperial ways. There would be no period of restoration to Russia's former glory. No reinstatement. The fallen would remain fallen. The poor would remain overlooked and taken advantage of. Justice would not be served. Now all that was left was a mad dash escape to friendlier soil.

An estimated one hundred and fifty thousand souls were rushing into the Caspian Sea or running towards the promise land of Constantinople. Refuge had been promised across the rough waters. The trouble was just surviving long enough to get there. The train stations were packed with fleeing citizens, farmers, peasants, gypsies, and soldiers alike. It was mad, and every person for themselves. Human decency had been left to the wayside. Screaming was rampant, crying even more so. Gunfire would not stop, and the artillery had everyone's mind in utter shambles. The city had been destroyed. The Reds and Blacks had their hands on just about everything these days. Those foolish enough to believe the Bolsheviks capable of such an emotion as compassion, and such a concept as mercy, were brutally executed. Lines of people were stood up against building walls and given little more dignity than an animal. Blood splattered everywhere, and colored everyone. Dead bodies littered the grounds, streets, parks, and beaches. Then the dead were further desecrated by being trampled upon, like a weed in the summertime. It was disgusting, but there was no time to stop and process anything. To stop was to die. So, everyone kept running, slamming into each other, and running some more. It didn't even matter what way you were running so long as you kept moving. Yoska was dragging Aanya by her left hand through the seaside city. He had no experience in the area, but he had ambitions to get to Odessa in the west, not far off from here. Behind the gypsy woman, green skirts flailing in the bitter and biting wind, she drug Dmitri by the hand. Claude brought up the rear, shooting all the way to keep them covered. He'd abandoned his blue uniform jacket for safety. Today was not the day to admit he was French. When he shot himself out of bullets, Claude was resourceful enough to check the bodies on the ground and pick up a new one, shoot it out, and repeat the process all over again. Yoska's running led the group of four to a beach, run red with bloody water and stained sands. Bodies floated like buoys in the sea, lapping up on each other and getting caught on the edges of boats. Every boat in the harbor, every boat in the proximity of Perekop, had been stuffed full of desperate refugees. People climbed up the sides like rats escaping floodwaters. Men propped up women, women propped up children, and sometimes even babies if they couldn't help themselves. It was madness. Life had come to this. Russia had fallen to a state of disrepair. And she'd done it to herself. The group was temporarily out of options, but a nearby ferry bound for Ukraine was currently taking paid reservations at eye gouging prices. Dmitri walked over to handle negotiations while Yoska and Claude sandwiched Aanya in-between them as they stood waist deep in the water to keep from being caught up in the swell of people on the beach, still trying to figure out what to do. As the waves ebbed and flowed, Yoska kept his hand on

Aanya's waist for good measure to make sure she was never swept out by a rogue wave. She too clasped her hand down on top of his, to keep herself in place as much as him. If any stranger had the bright idea of getting too close, Claude just shot them on sight, and after a few minutes, people started to get the idea. By the ferry Dmitri looked to be making progress with the operator, passing back and forth large sums of rubles. Aanya smiled genuinely for the first time in hours at the hope of getting out of here and safely back to Odessa where things might still make sense. She clutched a soaking hand onto Yoska's brown vest and pointed at the former Count.

"That's my man over there!"

"It sure is, Aanya."

"Do you think he'll have enough for all four of us? Do you think Dmitri will be able to whip a deal?"

"If there's any man that has enough money to buy us out of this mess right now, it's Dmitri."

"What do you think is taking so long?"

"They're probably haggling over a destination."

"You think Odessa is still safe right now?"

"It's close enough to be a good getaway, but far enough away that the Reds and Blacks won't be able to reach us on foot for at least a few days. By then we'll be on trains bound somewhere else."

"I sure hope you're right, Yoska."

"Don't worry, Aanya. We're going to be just fine."

She nodded her head and wrapped her arms around him before burying herself in his chest. They were both soaking wet, but he couldn't help but hug her tight. Her heart was racing a million miles a minute, but after he got his arms around her, she began to slow down. Dmitri came back, wading fastly, and insisted the ferry would drop them off at Odessa like they wanted before setting its sights on Constantinople, further to the south. The payment had been accepted at ten thousand rubles. Thankfully Dmitri had three times that amount on him, but the ferry operator was satisfied enough at ten. Unlike the other boats in the vicinity, this ferry had been highly selective in its passengers. Dmitri, his former countship not looked down upon amongst this company, was welcomed in among three dukes, two duchesses, and their children, a widowed countess, and several high society refugees who'd been sitting it out in this seaside escape for months now. Dmitri had managed to secure a whole room for the four of them to spend the night in. It was a crewman's locker, filled with a broom, tarps, and burlap sacks. But four people could sit down comfortably on the floor amongst all the hanging ropes on the walls. Dmitri had been lucky in locking this miniscule amount of privacy down, for a lot of other patrons were going to sleep on the deck tonight, in subzero temperatures with nothing else to shelter them but the clothes on their backs. They were fine clothes, the women in furs and the men in woolen suits, but it might not be enough. Aanya looked at them with sadness in her eyes as they exchanged relieved smiles between the lot of them. There was nothing anyone could do to help each other right now except for offering condolences and well wishes. But the latter seemed foolish with the constant thud of dead bodies hitting the outside of the ferry. In the closet of a room that Dmitri had secured, the four got cozy and tried to bundle themselves in such a way that the constant jostling of the sea would not impede their sleeping too much. Claude was out like a light, the first to start snoring, and the first to drop his guard. He still slept with a loaded gun propped up across his chest though. His arms held it in place like he was holding onto Mila. Aanya smuggled a giggle out under her breath, but the guys to either side of her could not reciprocate the gesture. Digging into his side, Yoska could feel Dmitri's coated arm around Aanya's waist as he held her close. Yoska wanted to hold her again like he had in the water, but the time for that had come and gone. What sat with him even worse in his own head, was that that might have been the last opportunity he'd have to hold her. He rolled to his side to face the wall but he could not sleep as Aanya and Dmitri whispered themselves into submission. Aanya always got chatty when she got nervous. It was an uncontrollable and albeit alluring quirk of hers. Dmitri was more than happy to keep her company as the ferry sailed for safer shores.

"What do you think will become of all of this when word reaches the big cities, Dmitri?"

"It's hard to say. I imagine it will be a difficult adjustment to know that the civil war has ended this way. Just cut off and truncated like this. A forced surrender by the Whites and Greens, I don't think it was in the public's best interest."

"Do you think Lenin will have reprisals for those who don't support him?"

"Are you worried about the camp being attacked again?"

"I am. With only Mila there to try and keep things together, I just don't know what's going to still be there, or who? I mean, we took a lot of the men down with us when we followed the Greens to Ukraine."

"The gypsies are a flexible and adaptable bunch. They know what they need to do to get by. They're survivors."

"It could be weeks before we get back up to Petrograd."

"We'll get there when we get there. There's really no rush. We have to be smart about this. With the Reds officially in charge now, this ferry ride might not be the only thing we have to buy our way onto."

"I feel so terrible about that."

"Don't. That's what I brought the money for in the first place."

"I don't want to see anything bad happen to you because people know you have it though."

"Nobody knows. As far as anyone else outside of this room is concerned, I gave everything I had to that operator. No one is going to come after me looking for more. But it is sweet of you to worry."

"I worry too much for my own good, I think."

"No. You worry a warranted amount."

"There were times this afternoon that I didn't think we were ever going to have moments like this again, just quiet and calm."

"I know what you mean. There were a few tough scrapes as we got through the city. But we made it. Yoska said we would."

"And you trust him?"

"I don't really have a choice in the matter."

"What do you mean?"

"You trust him with your life, with everything."

"He'd never do wrong by me."

"I know. And I have to respect that about him. We may have started out on the wrong foot he and I, but I'd like to think those days he held me captive in the forest are long behind us."

"You know he only went so far because he was trying to get a hold of me."

"I know. That man would do anything for you. Even if he didn't like it, if he thought there was even a chance that it'd make you smile, he'd do it. No questions asked."

"I feel guilty for inflicting such devotion."

"Don't. You have no control over how he feels, or how anyone else feels for that matter."

"I don't know what it is I control in general. It seems every time I try to hold onto something it just slips right through my fingers. It's all wrong. And it's been that way for over five years."

"It's over now."

"*Over*, over?"

"I think so. There's no coming back from a surrender, not like this. Hundreds of thousands are fleeing the country in any direction they can, while they still can."

"Do you think the Bolsheviks will try and stop the mass exodus of refugees?"

"I think they'll try, but I don't know how successful they'll be. Russia has a lot of borders to her name. They couldn't man them all. They might want to, but they don't have the manpower."

"In the dead of Winter too. That might be one thing the refugees still have on their side. People are more sympathetic when it's cold outside."

"You think so?"

"If it's a lie, let me believe it."

"Alright. I mean, it could be a good thing. I for one prefer to travel when there's *not* snow on the ground, or frozen waterways, but it could be an advantage to some people."

"How many people do you think are going to try and leave Russia when the Bolsheviks announce they've won the war?"

"Too many to count."

"With everyone running away, are we going to be the only fools trying to run back in?"

"No. I think there will be a decent amount of people looking to reconnect with loved ones before they flee. Refugees will want to stick together. When you're running for your life all you've got to your name is those people who share your name with you."

"I don't even know what I'd try to bring if I was running away."

"You don't?"

"I've tried not to think of such things."

"But I've been asking you to think about leaving Russia for months now."

"Leaving and running are two very different things, Dmitri. Leaving implies order, and civility. I'd be able to asses my things, say goodbyes, pack my belongings. Figure out what to do with little Ruslo, or bring him along."

"A fox on a train?"

"He's my best little friend. I couldn't leave without him! He's as loyal as they come."

"Alright. Assuming you have the time to bring Ruslo with you, what would you bring with you?"

"I'd pack my best clothes, my fine skirts and shawls. I have Gyorgi's fiddle. I'd have to take that with me. It's all I have of him. Come to think of it, I guess I don't have that many things to worry about. Nothing that can't be replaced."

"That's good to hear."

"Why is that good?"

"I've been holding onto something for a couple of weeks now. I've kept them with me just in case."

"Just in case what?"

"We happened to be the ones running away."

"What have you been keeping from me, Dmitri?"

"It's nothing bad. Just a couple pairs of tickets."

"Pairs of tickets?"

"For the group of us."

"Where to?"

"Paris. They're train tickets. Tickets to a new life."

"I didn't know you'd bought them already. I thought this was just something we were talking about and thinking over."

"No. I've been serious about this the whole time. *You've* been the only one holding back."

"Just because I've been holding back doesn't mean I haven't been serious too, Dmitri."

"I'm sorry for that. I know this is a big deal for you. I just figured if I bought the tickets and you knew how real this all could be, it might just be all the push you needed to accept this."

"I don't like being pushed into things."

"I know you don't. But this is for your own good."

"I'm a grown woman. I think I can tell for myself what is and isn't good for me."

"Please don't be upset with me."

"How could I not be upset right now? When were you planning on telling me we were leaving? The night before?"

"It was my original idea to surprise you on Christmas day. I thought it'd be a fitting present."

"Claude knew about this, didn't he?"

"He did. It was his idea to get us to Paris."

"Is that why he came down then? Not to join us in the fight, but to drag us back home so we could leave Russia altogether?"

"Yes. That is why he came down. It was his intention to spend Christmas in Paris this year, but I thought that might be too soon for you. I was hoping for new year's."

"You two are unbelievable!"

"Don't think Yoska didn't know about this too."

"He's been lying to me as well?!"

"All we've been trying to do was what was best for you, Aanya, and best for all of us in the long term. And that future hasn't been in Russia for quite a few years now. It lies somewhere else."

"Together at least?"

"Yes, you and me."

"That's not the together I was referring to. And you know it's not."

"People grow and they move on, Aanya."

"I don't want to move on. I want things the way they used to be when we were kids. Carefree, happy, and simple. I want my summers in the sunflower fields, Dmitri. I want my family and friends."

"A new life doesn't have to be devoid of that."

"But it will be different."

"Of course, it will be different. But it will be better. All of it will be better."

"Better is a matter of perspective."

10

Friday, 26th November

In the three weeks since the Reds claimed victory in the civil war there have been a rumored fifty thousand dissenters who've be trained off concentration camps and katorgas in Siberia. All that awaits those people is a slow and tortuous death by exhaustion, typhoid, cholera, or the flu. Suicide would be preferable to such a fate as disagreeing with the Bolshevik regime. To make matters worse for the public, there have been gas attacks carried out in the forests, and small inhabited areas on the outskirts of towns. The gas kills everyone indiscriminately, no matter what color army they may or may not have supported. Now if there is even the slightest hint of disapproval, it's worthy of death. Aanya, Dmitri, Claude, and Yoska arrived back up in Petrograd two days ago after their harrowing travels north. Yesterday Dmitri took the liberty of emptying his bank accounts, and gathering his two safes from his friends in town. The gypsy camp had been abandoned sans Mila, and her lone tent that she'd manage to hang onto. The Samoyed had packed Aanya and Dmitri's items, Claude's as well, and Gyorgi's fiddle. Ruslo had left though. The loyal little fox had chased the kids when they went running weeks ago. There truly wasn't anything left to hold onto in Russia now. The Red Army and Green Army had left the forest. Mila's only company lately had been the dead in the old campgrounds by the roads. She said she didn't mind, but her face betrayed her. It was cold outside, but not so cold to make her eyes as bloodshot as they were. She spent many hours of the day crying without shame of being heard. With the group back though she had to keep her emotions in check. She didn't have reason to cry with Claude back, smothering her with all the affection a man could possibly possess. That closeness just made Aanya intensely uncomfortable. Here she had Dmitri holding their future in his breast pocket, and there was Yoska, representing everything she was going to be leaving behind. He'd announced this afternoon he'd be going to Constantinople to try and rally the refugees for a comeback. Aanya knew he'd made this decision a while ago and only now had the nerve to break her heart. Under the light of a full moon the gypsy was going to make his final exit from Aanya's life, and she was finding herself unable to cope with the separation. Dmitri let Aanya walk Yoska to the train station alone for some much-needed privacy while the typically happy traveler had a courtesy train ticket bought for him by the Count, bound for Odessa. The train station was full of sad goodbyes and women crying and Aanya hated to be so stereotypically weak in her choice of emotions.

"Please don't cry, Aanya. You're not making this any easier on me."

"Good. I don't want this to be easy for you, Yoska. I still don't know why you can't just come with us when we go to Paris."

"Gypsies aren't very well liked out west."

"But I'll be there."

"But your gorgeous face can open doors mine never could. Trust me, it'll be better this way."

"I hate that everyone keeps telling me how much better life is going to be when I'm abandoning all I've ever known."

"You never have been one to embrace change. I tried to tell everyone you wouldn't understand."

"Then explain it to me."

"There's not enough time."

"All the more reason for you not to go!"

"I'm afraid I have to get on this train tonight, Aanya. But before I do, I've brought something for you."

"What's this?"

"A goodbye gift, to remember me by."

"Like I could ever forget you."

"Well, open it up. I want to make sure you like it."

"It's a…book?"

"It's a diary. That way you can write to me."

"Where will I send the letters?"

"Let me worry about that."

"I'm going to miss you so much, Yoska."

"I'm going to miss you too, but it's like you've always said, our timing has never been right."

"I thought we'd always be in each other's lives."

"We will be, in a way."

"I thought you told me wherever I'd go, you'd go?"

"In time, you never know. It could be that way again. Now just isn't the time."

"I wish I had your confidence in what lies ahead."

"You do have it. You have every part of me, Aanya, and you always will. This is only a temporary goodbye. I promise."

"You better not break this promise to me, Yoska."

"I wouldn't dream of it. And I *will* dream of you, *every* night. You will never leave my thoughts. I will keep you with me in whatever way that I can."

"They're calling for the passengers to board now. I guess that means I have to let you go."

"We will cross paths again, Aanya. Tell me you believe that. I need to hear you say that."

"I believe you, Yoska. We will meet again."

"And don't let that good for nothing Count of yours tell you otherwise, alright? Because if Dmitri thinks he's going to keep you all to himself then he's going to be rudely awakened when I show up on your doorstep one of these days. And if I ever get word that he's made you unhappy in *any* way, why, I'll swim across oceans to make sure you're happy again. How does that sound?"

"Wonderful."

"Good. I'm glad to have gotten you to smile one last time before I leave. But I've got to go now, alright?"

"Alright. Oh! And Yoska?"

"Yes?"

"I love you."

"I know you do. I love you too."

Aanya held onto Yoska so long that he had to run to catch the train after it had already started rolling. But he made it on and settled into his window seat comfortably enough for a man who was breaking inside. With all of the steam rising from the heat of the train, Aanya was unable to see up into the frosted glass to wave Yoska goodbye. She resigned to waving aimlessly until the train was out of sight, just hanging her arm up in the air. There were wives here, and mothers. They all had handkerchiefs and scarves to suppress their emotions. Aanya was unabashed in her tears now though, and dropped to a ball right there on the train platform, burying her head in her knees and rocking back and forth on her heels. The only sounds that escaped her were choked off gasps of air. Yoska was going to be safe making this move to the south. He was going to do good work and try to help good people. Soon Aanya and Dmitri would be out of Russia as well. Claude and Mila were coming with them. They were to be married in Paris once they arrived. Claude kept talking about the church out in the countryside that he'd picked out. His eyes glowed when he described all the possibilities that he and Mila would be taking advantage of. All these stories the past couple of days were swirling around Aanya's head as the train platform emptied out. The carriages rode off, the women walked away. Aanya was the last one, and only lifted her head after the snow began to fall. There was a muffled silence that took hold of the atmosphere, and made her head clear up. The white ice was accumulating on the tops of her arms as they rested on her knees. She could have sat there and watched herself just get consumed in a snow drift, but a pair of cautious feet behind her let her know she wasn't alone. Dmitri had a blanket in his hands that he dropped down around her shoulders. Then he carefully dusted the snow off of Aanya's arms, and smoothed out the wisps of her tousled black hair. He took time admiring how it fell over her bare, copper skinned shoulders, and trailed down to her midsection. Then he pulled the blanket in tight around her and held it closed for her as she remained in a ball. Snow fell on them both, but he didn't mind. He sat down in a ball too, eye to eye with his beloved.

"I should have known you would have followed me out here, Dmitri."

"It's not that I didn't trust you, Aanya. I just wanted to make sure you were safe. Besides, I knew you'd be needing somebody to hold you right about now."

"My head hurts."

"When we get back to our tent, I'll light a fire for you. A warm sleep will help."

"It's so empty back there."

"We have all that we need. There's no lack of support. Modest means has always suited the pair of us, hasn't it?"

"Yes. I guess it doesn't take much to make us happy. We are going to be happy again, aren't we?"

"I know you're hurting right now, and I won't even begin to try and understand. But it will be better soon. You'll see. Everything is going to pick up for us. We're going to make it better. And we *can* do that."

"Can I ask you something?"

"Anything."

"Do you think it would be alright if we left Russia before Christmas?"

"You don't want to wait and spend it here?"

"I think if I wait too long, I might not ever leave. The less I think about it the easier it will be for me to make peace with what's happening."

"I'll go into town tomorrow morning and see what I can do about the tickets then."

"That won't be too much trouble will it? Because if it is then…"

"It won't be any trouble."

"Thank you."

"Can I ask you something?"

"Anything."

"Why the sudden change of mind?"

"Sitting in that camp during the day is like being in a graveyard. All those matted down spots. I can still hear everyone talking and laughing. I can still see the stones where they used to light the big bonfires on special occasions. I can't be around that knowing I'll never see it again."

"We don't have to stay in the forest anymore if you don't want to. If it's too difficult, we can just find a place in Petrograd for a little while."

"We can?"

"Aanya, I have the money to give you anything you'd ever want if you were only brave enough to ask me for it."

"I don't want you to think of me like Lotte. I'm not my sister, you know."

"I'm well aware what kind of woman you are."

"I don't want you spending all your money on me trying to make me happy."

"Keeping a roof over our head is my responsibility."

"Do you think we can be safe in the city?"

"We're not necessarily safe anywhere in Russia. But the city will be easier to navigate than the forests, especially with all the gas attacks going around."

"It's only a matter of time before they come for us out there. I almost forgot about that. I'm sorry. But ever since Yoska told me he was leaving this afternoon; my head hasn't been quite right."

"You take all the time you need to get right. There's no rush."

"He gave me this diary before he left."

"That was nice of him."

"He told me it was so I could write him letters. But I don't know what good that will do. I have no idea where he'll be from day to day."

"I might be able to make sense of that for you."

"What do you mean?"

"I have some connections in high places. I gave Yoska a list of addresses this afternoon that he could write to. They're men who I'm going to stay in touch with. So, one way or another, we will be able to keep track of where Yoska is."

"That was really nice of you."

"I did offer him a chance to come with us, you know. It wasn't like I told him he wasn't welcome."

"He's told me more than once before that he can't stand seeing you hold onto me. I know he's got his reasons for walking away from me now, but that doesn't mean I agree with them."

"He's not really walking away from you."

"Dmitri, the pain I feel in my chest right now, is no different than the pain I felt in my chest when you walked away from me when I was sixteen. Alright? It hurts just the same. So, yes. He did walk away from me. He's gone. A train took him away no different than a train took you away. And, yes. Both of you made sweet promises to me that you would see me again. But waiting for you was unbearably difficult, and after all this, I don't know if I have it in me to wait for him to come back to me, in however many years it might take."

"Like I said before, there's no rush for you to try and process all of this. I'll be here for you no matter how long it takes."

"You deserve better from me."

"What do you mean?"

"You're giving me all of this patience, and bending to my every insecurity. What am I giving you in return to justify such a kindness?"

"Your love. Your unflinching support of me through the years. Your unwillingness to give up on me after all this time even though I gave you a million reasons to do just that."

"You're a good man. You've been easy for me to love and hold onto."

"You're the only person who has never questioned if I was a good man or not. Did you know that?"

"Many people idolize you. You have so many friends in the world who look up to you and who respect you. I am not the only one."

"You're the only one I can trust. And you're the absolute only person in the world, who has loved me for my flaws. You loved me when I was a nobody."

"You've always been a somebody to me."

"But when I was an orphan, you were my only friend in the world. All the other kids made fun of me for my pale skin."

"No, Dmitri. They used to make fun of you for how sunburned you used to get in the summer."

"They used to call me freckleface."

"Your face used to be covered! I remember that. But you outgrew them."

"I didn't outgrow you though."

"I never could understand why you clung onto me after all these years. *Me*, of all the people you could have chosen to love. Why me?"

"Why not you?"

"I'm far from special."

"You don't recognize how special you are. Or how humble, and good natured, and brave, and strong, and smart, and gorgeous you are."

"You think I'm all those things?"

"Oh, I could keep going. How long do you want to sit here in the snow? Because if I'm going to list off all of the things that I love about you, then we're going to be here for a while."

"You are so good to me. I just hope that I don't let you down."

"You couldn't ever disappoint me."

"I just fear that you've put me up on this pedestal. I'm almost too perfect in your eyes."

"Aanya, you are far from perfect. I've never accused you of such a thing. I wouldn't love you if you were perfect. That's so boring, and you are anything but boring."

"I should hope so! But I am starting to get cold."

"*Starting?*"

"Crying can stave off the cold pretty well."

"Well, I don't want to hear you cry for a very, *very* long time. You hear me?"

"I hear you."

"No, I mean that."

"I know you do. I know, Dmitri."

"God, it's a shame you're so upset right now because I literally have my stomach tied in knots just looking at you."

"You do?"

"I don't think I've been this excited in…god maybe my entire life. We're really doing this, Aanya. You and me. We're going to be taking our first steps together into our new life."

"Soon. But not yet."

"I know, I know. But still, just the thought of it. The freedom. I feel like I can reach out and touch it now. It's *really* real. You've made me the happiest man in the entire world by taking this step with me."

"I'm glad I could do that for you."

"I'm glad for *us*."

"I'm ready to go home now, Dmitri."

11

Two days ago, a train left Moscow for Paris. Now Aanya and Dmitri found themselves twiddling their thumbs on a late-night stroll through Berlin while the train resupplied. It was going to take the better part of two hours and while most passengers were resigned to sleeping in their cabin, Aanya needed to get out and stretch her legs. It also didn't help that her bunkmates were the highly enamored couple of Claude and Mila which had spend the last several hours in an on again off again love making spiral which was trying Aanya's patience. Dmitri's original tickets had been for two cabins, but the tickets had been for the last week of December. On Aanya's request to leave before the holidays, one room was all Dmitri could afford on such short notice. Not that he was lacking in money, but one hundred thousand rubles for two room seemed more than a bit excessive, even with the sudden influx of refugees streaming out of the east. There were thousands. Those with money were fortunate enough to barter passage on trains and ships. Those without the proper finances hitchhiked, rode horses, or walked. Aanya imagined most of the people she'd considered family for the past five years were among the latter group, walking if they could manage. Despite them not being her responsibility anymore, she still worried for them. They were at the top of her thoughts while Dmitri tried his best to be a decent tour guide. He'd been here countless times in his youth, and while 1920 Berlin was a far cry from 1901 Berlin, there was still plenty of charm left to be found. He and Aanya walked arm in arm down the Unter den Linden. The tree lined thoroughfare had some of Berlin's most prized buildings, including the Opera House, City Palace, Humboldt University, Zeughaus, Berlin Cathedral, Hotel Adlon, Brandenburg Gate, the statue of King Frederick II, and the charming Castle Bridge, which was where the tour halted under a black, starry sky over the River Spree. Aanya was in a black fur coat, an early Christmas gift to make her better look the part of Dmitri's upper crust reputation. Here the Engelhardt name was strong, and Aanya had been introduced as Frau, meaning wife. She smiled smugly, and dutifully, careful not to draw attention to her copper skin. As bundled up as she was it was easy to hide. Her bright green eyes had always stolen the show anyway. She was in awe of Dmitri's flawless hold of the German language, and felt inadequate in her own abilities stepping into this new life. Clinging to the edge of the concrete work on the bridge, she stared down into the gentle current beneath her as Dmitri was keen on snuggling into her side.

"What are you thinking about right now, Aanya?"

"You speak the language here so well. I never knew that about you."

"Yes, well there wasn't very many opportunities for me to speak German in Russia."

"I wonder what other hidden talents you have that I don't know about."

"Not many. You know me better than anybody."

"I don't know anything about the thirteen years you spent in this country."

"You never asked. And frankly, I didn't volunteer the information because I always thought it was a kind of sore spot for you."

"Did you enjoy it here?"

"Germany is a beautiful country."

"This street reminds me of the Nevsky Prospekt back home. All the big buildings and grand architecture."

"They are quite similar."

"Are all the cities here in Germany as pretty as Berlin at night?"

"No. I don't think so. But this was always one of my

favorite places to visit. We didn't come nearly as often as I would have liked."

"Why not?"

"Wilfred preferred to be a big fish in a little pond. He had many connections around his home in East Prussia, but here in the big city, he was like a guppy in an ocean."

"I think I would have liked to see him at such a disadvantage."

"He took me here on my first week in country."

"That must have been amazing to be here when you were seventeen."

"I didn't really enjoy it as much as I should have. I saw what you saw. The Nevsky Prospekt, all a glow with people. But you weren't here, and I was still quite homesick."

"You were?"

"It was not easy for me to adjust to my new life here. Once Wilfred realized how withdrawn I was, without a friend in the whole country, that's when he introduced me to Lotte."

"Was she good to you when you two were younger?"

"She was still a child! The age gap at first you see,

she was five. I was more of a nanny. She kept me busy while Wilfred was doing business.”

“I forget she was as young as she was. She always acted so much older. Maybe it was the natural born arrogance in her?”

“You didn’t seem to inherit any of that.”

“I was raised by my mother. Maybe if Lotte had been left with her mother in Africa, she would have been better off too.”

“We don’t have to talk about your sister if it’s going to make you too uncomfortable, Aanya.”

“No. It’s alright. You seemed to have known a different side to her, a much kinder side. It makes me feel better knowing that she was not as rotten to the core as our father was.”

“Just because you are a von Behrend by blood, it doesn’t mean you are doomed to become anything like him.”

“Keep telling me that. Your reassurances are very helpful when I am wallowing as much as I seem to be these days.”

“Being homesick will wear off once we get reestablished. I promise. After a couple of months, you will find yourself so busy with new people and new projects that you won’t have time to wallow.”

"I am eager to get started on this new life of ours."

"That's the first time I think I've heard you say such a thing."

"Do you think you would have the patience to teach me some of this German that you know so well?"

"We can practice here and there. I never knew it was something that you wanted to learn."

"My father was German. Half of my blood belongs in this country. I think I should be able to speak the language of my people. Don't you?"

"I think it would be a good hobby for you."

"Is it very hard to learn?"

"It's not at all like Russian."

"Neither are the gypsy languages, but I can speak those good enough."

"I never was that comfortable with those."

"You didn't need to be."

"No, not when I always had you by my side to translate for me."

"We've always been a good team, haven't we?"

"I always thought so."

"That's not going to change is it?"

"No. Why would you think it would?"

"You keep telling me how everything is going to change, and be better. But I don't want everything to change. I still want to be able to love you the way that I always have."

"We will grow into our new lives, but who we are won't ever change."

"Are you sure? A new city, a new country won't make us grow apart?"

"I don't think it's actually possible for us to grow apart, Aanya."

"You don't?"

"If we were capable of such a thing, we would have done so already."

"Are you laughing at me?!"

"Yes, I am. A little bit."

"What's so funny?"

"You really don't get how much I love you, do you?"

"What do you mean?"

"Aanya, leaving you was the hardest thing I've ever had to do in my entire life. I cried like a baby for weeks. And then every time a storm would pass by…"

"Every time a storm would pass by…what?"

"Do you know that every time I hear thunder it reminds me of you?"

"Why is that?"

"All those days in the summer when we'd be out of boarding school on break, those days in the sunflower fields were some of my favorite memories. The thunderstorms would float over, and it'd send everyone running back to camp for shelter, but not you and me. We'd stay out and get soaked. You'd dance in the rain, and I'd just sit there and stare at how pretty you were. But I was so afraid to tell you."

"Why were you afraid?"

"I didn't want to ruin the good thing we had going. You were my best friend, and for a long time, my only friend. I was worried, as independent and headstrong as you were, that if I got too close, it might scare you."

"The only way you can scare me is to leave me."

"I know that now. But when I was a boy, I didn't. I think I got the first glimpse of how much you loved me when I left in 1901. You were so upset, and I was so confused."

"Confused? How could you have not known I was breaking inside?"

"I mean, I knew you were going to be sad. Saying goodbye wasn't going to be easy, but you'd do it. I figured you'd forget all about me, move on. I never thought I'd see that bracelet again."

"I proved you wrong."

"I'm so glad that you did. You still don't know what that bracelet is for, do you?"

"I never needed to know. All that mattered was that you gave it to me, and I wanted to hold onto it as long as possible."

"Aanya, that's the key to the safes that carry all of my fortune."

"You trusted me with the potential to have millions of rubles when I was *sixteen*?"

"I loved you. And I knew you'd take care of the money if you ever found out about it. I thought Jaina knew more than she did. I wanted you to be well taken care of."

"You are too sweet sometimes."

"Just sweet enough for you though?"

"Are you still nervous around me?"

"I don't ever want to lose you. And call me superstitious, but I know about what Jaina did to Wilfred when they were younger. He tried to get her out of Russia to start a new life, and in the middle of the night while the train was resupplying, she left him."

"I will not make the same mistakes as my parents. I will step forward where they stepped back. I owe it to both of us to be better."

"It does me good to hear you say that."

"Is that why you've been holding onto me so tight this evening? Because you were afraid if you lost sight of me that I'd run away on you?"

"That is part of the reason. But I mainly just like to hold onto you for the sake of holding onto you. And if you even knew half of the things I've been saying in German tonight…"

"What sorts of things have you been saying?!"

"Nothing bad!"

"What sorts of things, Dmitri?"

"Well, to the one old couple at the train station, the man said how pretty you were, and he called you my wife. I stretched the truth a bit and said we were traveling on our honeymoon."

"And to the young artist who was on the sidewalk?"

"He wanted to know if he could sketch us, me and my wife. He said he'd never drawn a woman so pretty before and promised he'd do a good job."

"And the carriage driver?"

"He was trying to get me to pay for a ride through town because my wife must be exhausted. And a fine woman like you should not have to walk if she does not want to."

"They all assumed I was your wife?"

"I guess they can tell how in love I am by the way that I look at you."

"Or by the way I look at you."

"Maybe a little of both?"

"You make the people here sound so friendly."

"Despite what the Russians might say, Germans are actually very fine people."

"I wonder what a life here might look like?"

"If we didn't go to Paris, you mean?"

"Well, we have to go to Paris. I botched your plans once; I can't very well do it again."

"You can botch them as many times as you want."

"Claude and Mila are to be married in Paris. In that countryside little church that he keeps going on about. I swear, if I have to hear about how pretty the flowers are in Springtime…"

"He does sound really happy to be going home, doesn't he?"

"He's been painting a good picture for Mila."

"As good a picture as I've been painting for you, I hope?"

"You've never told me if we were going to stay in Paris after their wedding."

"That's because I was leaving that decision up to you. This isn't just my future, it's ours. And I want you to have a say in where we go."

"What if I don't know?"

"Then we'll figure it out together, in our time, just like we do everything else."

"You sure do have a lot of faith me."

"Shouldn't I?"

"Yes. It's just a lot of responsibility."

"Well, I guess I'm lucky you're good at that sort of thing then, huh?"

"You smile like a little kid when we talk about our future. All wide eyed and glowing."

"Is that a bad thing? I can try to tone it down a bit if I'm embarrassing you."

"Smile like a fool. I never have been nor will I ever be embarrassed of you. It's just, that damned smile of yours in contagious, and it makes me smile like an idiot too. Then my cheeks start shaking and I wonder if this isn't all a perfect dream I might have to wake up from."

"This is no dream. This is really happening."

"I mean, we're in Berlin right now! Isn't that just a little bit crazy after the past five years?"

"Crazy in a good way."

"This city is gorgeous. The people are nice. They went through war. Why did Russia have to be so ruthless about everything? Why did they have to go and make life so hard?"

"So, you're beginning to see it then?"

"See what?"

"That a life outside of Russia can be good."

"I'm beginning to see it. And I'm so glad you pushed me when I didn't think I needed it. I'm so lucky to have a man like you at my side."

"When we get to Paris, we can talk about where to go from there. I'll hold off buying tickets until then. And don't worry about the logistics or the money or any of the petty details. I'll take care of everything. I'm going to take good care of you, Aanya."

"I know you are, because you're too good of a man to go back on your word. And I'm too in love with you to let you go."

"*Too* in love. I like the sound of that."

"I thought you would."

"We should probably start heading back for the train now. We don't want them to leave without us."

"Do you think Claude and Mila have calmed down?"

"I hope so. But if not, we just might have to fight fire with fire tonight. If you're up to it?"

"I thought you'd never ask!"

12

Saturday, 25th December

France was still early in her rebuilding years. Paris was a sight to see regardless. For the first few days upon arriving in the adopted homeland of the former peace ambassador, Claude was the tour guide of all tour guides. He carted his friends dutifully around all of his old haunts. The bakery was a hot spot they hit every morning. Mila was in heavenly bliss as she was carted on the arm of her beloved fiancé. Aanya and Dmitri too were in quite good spirits. The holidays were decorated well in the streets, with festive happiness in no short supply. France had suffered significantly for rh four years they endured the Great War. Aanya remembered all the stories from the Western Front in the streets of Petrograd and in the papers. She'd always been so happy to be so far away, but she was not removed anymore. On the train ride she saw the war-torn fields and hillsides. There were forests reduced to match sticks, and once smooth fields cratered to bits by artillery. Trenches were carved into the landscape with the most gruesome barbed wire blockades. Little crosses had been popped up all over the place. Wherever a soul fell. There were thousands upon thousands. The crosses appeared to grow like weeds. And there was the human toll as well. Men struggling on crutches with an amputated leg. Amputated arms were quite common to see on the streets. The amputees were always the friendliest of men. They'd tip their hats and bow at Aanya and Mila. Very gentlemanly, very proper. Manners and human kindness had not deteriorated her like in Russia. What survived in the east through the Great War did not survive the Civil War.

Today was Christmas morning. Frost covered the ground in a fine white layer of ice, just enough to shoot off rainbows for a few brief moments at sunrise before the heat melted the earth. Aanya had a steaming cup of tea in her hands as she stared out the window. She'd always been an early riser, no matter where she was. Dmitri noticed the bed was cold beside him when he rolled over, and was quick to resume his place at Aanya's side, wrapping him around her from behind, and snuggling his face into her neck until she giggled like a teenager. He took a sip of her tea over her shoulder and nestled into comfortable complacency. After whispering Merry Christmas in her ear, they both released massive matching grins and couldn't believe where they were. In the little country town just outside the main vein of Paris, La Queue-en-Brie was sleepy on a holiday. There were green hills outside Claude's apartment window. It was a single-story little hobble of a home, but it was quaint and cozy and two bedroomed. That was an important distinction. The exterior was creamy white like the froth of fresh milk and the grass was unbelievably lush and green with little daisies growing everywhere. Aanya imagined what the hills looked like in Spring, with all the colors of the rainbow-like Claude had been describing for weeks. It would be a nice life here. Aanya could imagine hanging laundry on a line between the little trees, and having children laughing in the yard. It was nothing like back in Russia, but that was a good thing. Such peace of mind, it made breathing easier. But today was going to be a big day. Claude and Mila were to be married!

Claude's church of choice was an ancient relic of the little town. It'd been built in the eleventh century, and truly had stood the test of time with it's gray brick walls and church steeple standing tall amongst the grassy hills. It was the St. Nicholas Church. It had a planked wooden front door that was rounded on top, with metal bracing straps running across it. Inside the wooden pews looked like they had been hand hewn hundreds of years ago. There was a charm to the craftmanship. Because the wedding was so intimately small, and the church fairly decent in size, there was an echo to every motion that took place. Every step had a hush to it, every whisper spoken in confidence to a lover, amplified. To hold such an event on a holiday meant special arrangement so as to not interfere with normally scheduled masses when the crowds came in. That mean Claude and Mila were getting married oddly early, just after sunrise. It would be quick, without all the fuss of usually ornate ceremonies.

That was fine though, if not preferred by the happy couple. Claude had no family to invite. Mila had her sisters, but there was no need to go bothering them in Siberia with her new life. She loved them, but to tell them of her staggering good fortune now would only seem vastly inappropriate what with all of the hardships befalling Russia right now. Dmitri and Aanya were all the witnesses required or wanted. Since rubles were no good in France, there was an exchange of gold to buy the preacher's good services, and for a set of rings for the happy couple. Dmitri also bestowed fine clothes on the four of them. For the men, fine brown suits, and for the bride a dress of lilac, Mila's favorite color. Aanya wore a rotten green, form fitting dress hung just above her knee, reminiscent of the color of her fraying ribboned bracelet. The green of her dress also made her eyes pop, which Dmitri was quite fond of. As Claude and Mila said their vows to one another, it was Dmitri could do to keep his mouth shut, because the man was deeply inside of his own head, and his cheeks were flushed as bright red as if he was the one getting married today. Once the wedding was over Dmitri had bought two carriage rides to parade down the Champs-Élysées, which was essentially the whose who of avenues in Paris, no different than Berlin's Unter den Linden, and Petrograd's Nevsky Prospekt. Aanya was in wide eyed wonder, playfully gripping onto Dmitri and pointing wildly at all the sights and sounds. She shouted at the Arc de Triomphe, among other famous buildings. Her excitement made Dmitri laugh, but Aanya was not so caught up in the day's events that she couldn't tell he was a bit off.

"Dmitri? You've been stuck up inside of that handsome head of yours for hours now. What's wrong?"

"Nothing's wrong."

"Dmitri. I know you better than you know yourself. Just say what it is you've been wanting to say."

"Would it be terribly rude of me to steal Claude and Mila's thunder?"

"What do you mean?"

"It's their wedding day, and I know this day should be all about the two of them, but when they were in that church saying their vows, I just couldn't help but think how badly I wanted that to be you and me standing up there."

"It will be one day."

"It will?"

"Assuming you scrounge up enough courage to ask me properly."

"I've been trying all morning."

"Any words you have for me will be the right ones. You don't need to overthink it."

"But you deserve the world. How could I possibly explain how much I love you and how hopeless I would be if I couldn't spend the rest of my life with you?"

"Just like that."

"So, you *will* marry me?"

"Yes."

"I figured you'd say yes, but it feels even better than I imagined! It's funny, isn't it? Just a short little word like that, and I've heard you say it a million times at least, but never with so much love behind it."

"You're so funny when you're nervous."

"I think I sound like a rambling idiot."

"Then you can be *my* rambling idiot."

"You'd take me as I am? Mess and all?"

"I took you when you were little more than a poor, freckle faced orphan. Isn't that what those vows are all about? In sickness and in health, for richer or poorer. I love you all the same. I loved you in Russia, in Germany, and now in France."

"And where will you love me next?"

"I don't know. I haven't decided."

"Might I make a suggestion?"

"Of course."

"I've been talking with some of my friends that have made it out to London."

"London, England?"

"Doesn't light your fire?"

"I'm a little dark skinned for them up in the north, aren't I?"

"I wasn't planning on going to England. But there has been much anticipation surrounding the United States."

"That seems so far away."

"All the more reason to consider it, don't you think?"

"It's about as far from Russia as you could get."

"It was just a suggestion."

"What did you friends say about the United States? Did it sound promising?"

"They've been closed to immigrants from the start of the war all the way to last year. But they're open again, and there's supposed to be many opportunities for European refugees like you and I."

"We'd be going alone, wouldn't we?"

"I think Claude has made it more than obvious he desires to plant roots here in La Queue-en-Brie."

"If you think this is a lead we should take advantage of, then buy the tickets."

"Really?! I mean, are you sure? You don't want to think it over any longer?"

"You've never led me astray before. There's no reason to think you would now. I'll follow you absolutely anywhere."

"This is going to be a fun life, you know that?!"

"I'm excited."

"I am too!"

"How soon would we be going?"

"That depends. I'll send a letter out this afternoon to my friend, and see what he can do. If he needs us to act sooner rather than later, would that be alright?"

"That'd be ideal."

"I can't believe it! We're really going to do this!"

"We're really doing it."

"God, I love you! Have I told you how much I love you today, Aanya?"

"Only about a million times."

"Shoot! Then I'm behind."

"You're ridiculous!"

"Ridiculously in love with you!"

"If this is what you're going to be like when we move to the United States then I'm going to have my hands so full with you, aren't I?"

"I would hope so. Because I have *every* intention of keeping my hands full of you."

"Dmitri!"

"I love it when you say my name like that."

"Like what?"

"You have this squeaky little way you laugh when I grip onto you and surprise you. I absolutely love it."

"I didn't even know that I did that."

"There is so much you don't realize."

"Is there ever a moment when you're around me that you're not staring at me?"

"No. When I'm with you, why would I want to bother looking at anything else?"

"You're hopeless!"

"You're no better!"

"No, I'm not. What have we turned into? Are we as sickeningly sweet as all those lovesick couples we've seen before?"

"Maybe we're worse."

"We would be, wouldn't we? There's never any form of moderation when it comes to you and me. All or nothing, black or white, up or down."

"Here or there, but never in-between."

"Ugh! *Never* in-between. Not us!"

"I think I've heard you laugh more this morning than I have in the past five years combined."

"And all it took was getting me out of that frozen hell hole we used to call a home."

"It wasn't all bad."

"No. It was beautiful. But the people became so ugly. The establishment and their rules. It's not like that in the United States is it?"

"No. From everything I've heard it is the land where dreams come true. Hard work is rewarded and they take in people from absolutely everywhere. It's the safe haven of all safe havens."

"It is the place to start a family, then?"

"Have you been thinking about having children?"

"I don't know if I can have them, but I sure would like to try. This morning when I was looking out that window, I swore I could hear kids laughing on those green hills. I want that for us. For you and me. I want that fresh start. I want to raise up little ones, and give them the whole world. I want to give them everything we didn't get to have."

"You will be a wonderful mother."

"You think so? You don't think I would be too…abrasive or something?"

"You don't give yourself enough credit. Just because you are a strong woman doesn't also mean you're not the most caring, and empathetic woman I've ever met. Not to mention gorgeous."

"I think you'd be a good father too."

"Really? Even if I didn't have one myself?"

"You know everything not to do. All you have to do is be yourself, and you'll be golden."

"You're biased, Aanya."

"Unregrettably so."

"I'd be lying if I said I hadn't thought about having kids too. I just didn't know how to bring it up to you. Claude told me the other day he thinks that Mila might be pregnant already."

"I wouldn't doubt it! The way those two are. She hasn't said anything to me though."

"She hasn't said anything to Claude either. He just knows. He said he knew his wife was pregnant with their daughters when he was younger before she ever did. I'd like to think he's right about that."

"Because you want Mila to be a mother?"

"Because I want you to be one too."

"I thought we were talking about Claude and Mila here, not you and I."

"He said he thinks you might be pregnant too."

"I think he's too wishful in his thinking."

"You're not very far along he said."

"If this was true, and he has this…sixth sense, then he would have caught me in my lies two years ago when I…"

"He knew then. He just didn't say anything."

"He knew I lost the baby too?"

"Which is why he continued not to say anything."

"He's a good man."

"One of the best."

"I'm going to miss them when we leave."

"We'll write to each other. We have his address, and soon enough we'll have one of our own too. And we'll be able to visit each other as often as we can."

"Do you really think he's right, Dmitri?"

"About what? Staying in touch?"

"No! About me being pregnant? Could I be?"

"I mean, scientifically speaking, there's been many, *many* chances for you to get pregnant. The likelihood of one of our late-night rendezvous being the act that sealed the deal is pretty high."

"Do you think I'm going to lose the baby again?"

"No. I don't."

"Why not? Why would this time be any different than last time?"

"Because this is you and me. This is *our* baby. And I'm going to take good care of you and make sure nothing, and I mean *nothing* gets in the way of us having the best life possible."

"Would you love me any less if you found out that I lost it though?"

"No. Not at all. If anything, that'd just give us another opportunity to try again. And we'll keep trying as much as you want. If not, we can adopt. Or we can get animals. We can take in stray cats! Feed the sparrows in the trees! Aanya, no matter what, I'm living a full life with you, whatever that might look like. I want the full experience. I want to know what it's like to live my highest highs with you and my lowest lows. I want it all. I'm a greedy, greedy man when it comes to you."

"I'm greedy too. Dmitri, I want to marry you."

"We are going to get married."

"But I mean, I want to marry you soon. Today."

"*Today*?"

"Do you think you could pay the preacher to marry us back in Claude's church?"

"You don't have to ask me twice. Driver? Driver?! Turn around. We're in need of a church. Now!"

13

Three days ago, Aanya and Dmitri said goodbye to mainland Europe, their friends in France, and all the life they've ever known. This morning they arrived in the port city of Southampton, England. Dmitri was meeting his friend from Warsaw who had made a small fortune the past few months getting refugees out of Eastern Europe. The two men went back to their twenties when they were both upcoming men in high society. They'd both done fairly well for themselves and had kept in touch with one another on a fairly regular basis. The man's name was Jerzy Savchenko. He had slicked back black hair and a prominently crooked nose square in the middle of his ling face. His suit cost more money than Aanya could even dream of holding in her hands at one time. He smelled of rich alcohol and cigar smoke. She looked at the clock on the wall, it was only eight in the morning. Aanya kept a tight grip on Dmitri's bicep as he laughed off her nerves in friendly company. Jerzy tipped his head towards her to imply he meant no ill will. He was a tall man, slender in stature, and intimidating, but much less so when a slim grin peeled across his face. It didn't stay there for long, but she appreciated it. Jerzy lost further strength in appearance when his six-year-old son came running out from deeper in the seaside office and clung onto his father's leg. The boy looked nothing like him, red hair and freckles, round framed glasses. He hid behind his father's thigh as Aanya giggled, and then she bent down to be eye to eye with the little one.

"And what might your name be, sir?"

"It's alright. Tell the pretty lady your name son."

"My name is Paweł."

"Well, it's very nice to meet you, Paweł. My name is Aanya."

"Aanya? That's a funny name."

"No, son. That's not nice to say."

"I'm sorry, Aanya."

"No, it's alright. Paweł how old are you?"

"I'm this many."

"Oh, you're six. You must be in school by now?"

"Papa teaches me."

"Your papa must be very smart."

"He's the smartest papa I know."

"Aanya?"

"Yes, Dmitri?"

"Would you like to stay and chat with Paweł for a little while so Jerzy and I get things settled?"

"Sure. No problem. Um, can I trouble you Jerzy for some spare paper and pens?"

"Of course. Here you go."

"Thank you so much. Paweł, do you like to draw?"

"I'm a really good drawer!"

"Tell me what's the best thing you can draw?"

"I can draw people. Mama, papa, me, and Karol."

"Who's Karol?"

"Our cat!"

"Can you draw Karol for me? What color is Karol?"

"You've got yourself a good woman there, Dmitri. I always knew you'd settle down with a fine wife."

"Thanks, Jerzy."

"Is this the infamous gypsy you used to talk so much about when we were younger?"

"She is."

"She's even prettier in person."

"No words could do that woman justice."

"You two don't have any children of your own yet?"

"We're working on it."

"She'll be a good mother. I can tell by the way she latched onto my son so fast. Paweł can be such a handful sometimes, but she jumped right in. You be sure to keep a close eye on that one or another man might just come along and try to take her off your hands for you."

"No. That's not possible. For some reason she thinks the world of me."

"You?! Does she know you?!"

"Alright, alright! You've had your fun. Now how do those tickets look?"

"I just got them in last night. Two tickets for New York's Ellis Island. Just like you asked."

"Perfect. And when does our ship leave?"

"Boarding doesn't start until noon, and the ship sets sail just before sundown at five."

"Thank you for doing this for me on such short notice."

"It's fine. I had a couple back out right before you sent me a letter."

"Might I ask why they backed out on such a good deal?"

"Turns out the little wife found out about a mistress the husband had set up already in New York."

"No!"

"He wanted to have his cake and eat it too. The wife wasn't about to step into that mess."

"One man's misstep is another man's opportunity."

"Something like that."

"Are you good here in Southampton, Jerzy?"

"Good enough."

"Why is a man as smart as you still playing with immigration tactics when he could be a businessman in the United States?"

"My wife is pregnant right now, and doesn't want to travel until after the baby is born."

"Congratulations."

"Thank you. I think."

"You think?"

"She's having a real rough go at it this time around. That's why she's not here with me right now. I took our boy with me to try and make things easier on her. I'll be headed back to Warsaw next month. You caught me just in time."

"I wish you and your family all the best."

"I do too. I envy you, Dmitri."

"You envy me, Jerzy? Whatever for?"

"A brand-new start, a woman who's willing to follow you anywhere you go. Nothing's holding you down."

"You feel restrained in life?"

"Even after my wife has the baby, there's the issue of my mother. She's as stubborn as they come. She stayed in Warsaw during the war, through the

German occupation and everything. She was born in that town and she is determined to die in that town."

"Aanya gave me a lot of trouble at first too. All she's ever known is Russia. She didn't want to leave."

"But she's here now."

"Yes. She sure is."

"You smile like a fool when you look at her."

"If she was yours, wouldn't you smile like a fool too?"

"That I would."

"When we get settled in the United States, I'll be sure to write to you again with our new address. Should I send it to your offices here or in Warsaw?"

"You can write to the university actually."

"University?"

"I've got a new job starting this Spring at the University of Warsaw."

"I never would have thought the man who introduced me to the night life of East Prussia would ever be trusted with teaching the youth of the next generation."

"Well, that's the university's mistake, now isn't it?"

"I'm just giving you a hard time, Jerzy. I think you'll make a wonderful teacher. What classes might you be in charge of?"

"I don't know yet. They're still getting me settled into a department. I asked for History but they're in need of a Political Professor."

"Who better to tackle international relations than a smuggler of people?"

"Yes. But I didn't come clean to them about all of this backdoor business that I'm doing right now. It's just to pay the bills in these lean times."

"They are lean, aren't they?"

"Have been for some time now."

"It must be even harder for you with such a young family."

"Keeping Paweł in glasses is going to make me go broke if he doesn't stop breaking them every two weeks."

"A wild child like his father no doubt?"

"Not something I'm particularly fond of."

"He must look like his mother though."

"Yes. She's the prettiest redhead I've ever seen."

"Might I ask you for some advice?"

"About what? Wives? I think you've already got me beat in that department!"

"No, about being a father."

"Are you nervous?"

"You know I never had a father of my own. I'm afraid Aanya's going to be depending on me to raise a family and I might let her down because I have no idea what I'm doing."

"Relax. No parent ever knows what they're doing."

"Really?"

"We all make mistakes, Dmitri. The important thing is that the child knows they're loved, and that they're safe. It really is true what they say, that it takes a village to raise a child. You and Aanya won't be in this alone."

"We have no family or friends in the United States."

"You will soon enough. Trust me. Everything will work out. You always were the lucky one out of the two of us."

"I was, wasn't I?"

"And with a woman like Aanya at your side, you'll have friends in no time. My son is so painfully shy around strangers, and look at the two of them right now sitting at the table. You'd swear those two were lifelong friends."

"She's always been good with kids."

"Not everyone is."

"It's the gypsy in her. She's used to being part of a crowd. And I've taken her away from all of that."

"You'll find a new crowd. You're giving her a once in a lifetime opportunity here. Don't beat yourself up over this. You have nothing to be guilty about. If my circumstances were any better, I'd be joining you in a heartbeat. But once again, our paths have merely crossed, Dmitri, they haven't merged."

"You'll always be welcome at my home, Jerzy, wherever that might be."

"Thank you. I'm going to hold you to that invitation when my wife and I get overwhelmed with the kids and need a vacation. Can I dump my mother on you as well?!"

"The more the merrier!"

"I wish I had your life, Dmitri."

"Yours sounds like it turned out pretty well."

"A man always wants what he cannot have though."

"With your slick talking connections, I find it hard to believe anything you want remains out of your grasp for very long."

"You'd be surprised."

"You're not in any kind of trouble, are you Jerzy?"

"Not yet!"

"I'm serious. I have money if you need some help."

"I could never take a handout from you. It wouldn't be right."

"Friends help friends. How much do you need?"

"Dmitri, I really can't."

"It would make me feel better if I left you with something. Now come on, name a price."

"You wouldn't happen to have a few thousand rubles burning a hole in your pocket, now would you?"

"How does ten sound?"

"Dmitri I couldn't. That's too much!"

"Consider it a gift for the new baby then. This is five from me and five from Aanya. Will that sit better with your conscience?"

"You don't need to talk it over with your wife first?"

"Do you really want to involve my wife in this affair?"

"Why? Would that be a bad idea?"

"For you it would be. She'd probably insist that you took twenty from us."

"She's so generous with money?"

"She's never had any money to her name. It means nothing to her. People are what hold value."

"Then as long as she's with you she's as rich as they come, isn't she?"

"She didn't marry me for my money."

"What did she marry you for?!"

"I have things to offer a woman!"

"I know you do. I just wanted to leave on a high note. I'll do my best to visit you as soon as I can. Maybe sometime this Summer?"

"That would be nice. I'll keep an eye on the mail."

Jerzy put his hand out for a shake. Dmitri took it but only to pull his friend in for a hug. From their makeshift arts and crafts table Aanya and little Paweł saw this closing gesture and invited themselves back into the main room of the office. Jerzy picked up his son and held him on his side like a proud father as Dmitri pulled onto into his side like a proud husband. Both men then marveled at the other's achievements, tipped their heads and bid a bittersweet farewell to one another. At the door an antsy Paweł had to run after Aanya and hug her too before she was gone for good. Dmitri chuckled to himself thinking how perfect his life was going to be. He was sure Aanya was pregnant now. Claude had planted that seed in his mind and it was going to stick until he got the evidence he so required. First thing first Dmitri had to get them into a house, with a yard. He'd promised Aanya sunflowers, so that's what she was going to get. A whole field of them, just like back home. She needed a roof over her head, and room for the baby to be comfortable. Dmitri would go broke chasing their dreams, and he couldn't be happier at the prospect of a quiet, simple life out in the country somewhere. He'd get his stationary in order, and write letters to everyone to come and visit. He tapped on the tickets in his pocket frequently, to make sure he didn't lose them on the way down to the harbor. At noon they'd be among the first in line to board, and by sunset they'd be on the bow, looking off in to the horizon, and their future. He couldn't stop smiling. It was an infectious kind of happy that Aanya so tickled with excitement she barely had an appetite for her late morning tea.

"Might I see those tickets of ours, Dmitri?"

"Oh! Um, yes. Yes, of course."

"Did I startle you, or something? Are you as lost in thought as I am?"

"I can't get over how well you did with Jerzy's son this morning."

"He was a cute little boy. Wasn't he?"

"Our children will be cute too. I hope they look just like you."

"Just like me? Um, Dmitri, did…"

"You saw our names on the tickets, didn't you?"

"Dmitri and Aanya *Engle*?"

"I figured it'd be harder for Russia to chase us if we assumed a bit of a new identity for ourselves. Do you like the sound of it?"

"*Mrs. Engle*. I do rather like the way that it slips off of the tongue."

"I'm rather fond of the way you say it too. *Mrs*. My *Mrs*. though. All mine."

"The *Engles*. Yes. I could get very used to that."

www.ingramcontent.com/pod-product-compliance
Lightning Source LLC
Chambersburg PA
CBHW031302160726
47993CB00001B/272